Shadowverse

JASON J. HAYWARD

Dedicated to...

Nancy – My "It Girl," yesterday, today, and forever.

Peyton – My "Crew" since day one. Never lose that spark; it's going to take you to the moon and back.

Kitsune – The most talented artist I've ever known. Keep that light in your eyes and love in your heart.

Thank you all for the love, the laughter, and the memories!

Contents

CHAPTER ONE

Journey to the Unknown

Ryan McFarlane sat uncomfortably in the back of the taxi, his gaze fixed on the endless wave of cars ahead. The honks, the cacophony of engines, everything about Los Angeles traffic annoyed him. He checked his watch again, his heart pacing with the ticking second hand - his flight to Tokyo was in less than two hours.

"I really don't want to do this", he muttered under his breath, his fingers tapping a staccato rhythm against the worn leather of the car seat. Japan was never on his bucket list, its foreign customs and language only served to heighten his anxiety. Plus, leaving meant two weeks away from his already crumbling marriage. Not that his wife Allie McFarlane, a pretty, yet bitter woman with a permanent scowl, was any comfort to be around. Still, he was not ready to give up on his marriage. Not just yet. The timing for this business trip to Tokyo could not have been worse.

He pulled out his phone, contemplating sending her another message. The last text he sent, lamenting his departure, was met with silence. The strain between he and Allie was nearing its breaking point, but Ryan, ever the optimist, continued to try, hoping for a semblance of warmth. However, his optimism was usually met with cold indifference.

As the taxi inched closer to LAX, a knot of dread formed in Ryan's stomach. He was about to embark on a journey to a land he had no interest in, leaving behind a broken relationship with a hope for reconciliation that seemed to be diminishing with every passing second. Little did he know, Tokyo was about to change his life in ways he could never have imagined.

Just as the sun began to set, dyeing the sky with hues of crimson and orange, Ryan finally reached Los Angeles International Airport. He hurried through the bustling crowds, his suitcase trailing behind him, echoing his anxiety with its restless wheels. The routine of security checks did little to ease his nerves. He took off his shoes and belt, unpacked his laptop, and watched as his essentials disappeared into the black hole of the X-ray machine. Once through, he retreated to the refuge of his chosen gate, his heart still pounding, his mind filled with apprehension.

Sitting alone amidst the sea of faces, he stared blankly at the massive Airbus A380 that awaited its passengers. His hands felt cold and clammy, his stomach churned with a cocktail of dread and despair. Then, his phone buzzed, tearing him away from his reverie. It was his wife. "Have a good trip," she voiced blandly, the words sounding more like an obligation than a genuine sentiment.

Ryan, however, seized the opportunity, his voice cracking with restrained emotion. "Listen, I know things have been rough...and I know I'm not perfect. But I promise to work on it. We can fix this," he pleaded, his voice echoing his desperation. There was a pregnant pause, a silence that seemed to span an eternity before she responded, "Have a safe flight." with a voice devoid of any emotion.

His heart sank, a sharp, stinging sensation of rejection searing through him. He hung up, a lump forming in his throat, a stamp of the heartbreak he was trying to suppress. Boarding began, and he trudged onto the packed plane, the sounds of excited chatter and crying babies fading into a meaningless buzz. As he settled into his window seat and peered out the window he was unable to shake off the loneliness that crept into his heart, a harsh reminder of the distance that now strained his marriage, in both the figurative and literal senses. Little did he know, this was just the beginning of his journey, a journey that was about to change his life in the most unexpected ways.

CHAPTER TWO

A Rain Soaked Reception

The massive Airbus a380 finally touched down in Tokyo, its wheels skidding slightly on the rain-soaked runway. As the plane taxied slowly up to its designated spot at the terminal, Ryan looked out the window with the gnawing feeling of homesickness setting in.The late hour and stormy weather only made it worse.

His phone, that trusty companion, now decided to betray him, refusing to connect. All he wanted was to send a simple text - "Arrived in Tokyo" - a silent plea for some semblance of normalcy amidst the alien surroundings. Annoyance bubbled up inside him as his attempts to restore the connection proved futile.

Seeing his fellow passengers finally filing off of the plane, he pocketed the stubborn device, hoisted his backpack onto his shoulder, and made his way through the lonely, winding corridors of Tokyo's massive Narita airport. After a short interview at customs, he was on his way. Outside, the night was dark and quiet, the usually bustling curb now just a deserted stretch, slick with rain.

A lone taxi stood at the curb, its headlights cutting through the darkness and illuminating the steadily falling raindrops. Ryan approached, relief washing over him that he wouldn't have to wait for a car. He used the five or so Japanese words he knew with the driver, his broken pronunciation earning a chuckle from the driver, before getting in. As the taxi pulled away from the airport and slid onto the rain-slicked streets, Ryan pressed his forehead against the cool window, Tokyo's neon lights blurring in his vision. The realities of his isolation were setting in, but so too was the unfamiliar thrill of a new city, a new beginning. His earlier feelings of homesickness slowly fading away.

The taxi pulled up in front of the Park Hyatt Hotel, a towering beacon of light in Shinjuku's skyline. Ryan paid the driver, thanked him for the ride, and made his way into the grand lobby. The staff welcomed him warmly. Their professionalism and kindness impressed him. They quickly checked him in and directed him to his room.

His suite was on the 42nd floor, offering a breathtaking view of Tokyo's cityscape. He stood by the window, mesmerized by the sea of twinkling lights. But as he unpacked his belongings, a wave of jet lag hit him. Physically, he was exhausted, but when he gave up on packing to lay down and get some sleep, he was unable to. He was just too wound up, the adrenaline of being in a new city keeping him awake.

Deciding to take advantage of his insomnia, Ryan left the hotel and ventured out into the streets of Shinjuku. He was instantly swept up in the bustling energy of the neighborhood. Ignoring the sporadic drizzle, he started to look for a place to eat. After wandering a bit, he stumbled upon a small, inviting ramen shop.

Just as Ryan was about to enter the ramen shop, a smiling man approached. His name was Kazu Sato, his sleek suit bearing a stark contrast to the casual attire of the crowd around them. Ryan, oblivious to the world of Yakuza and their reputation, engaged in conversation with Kazu. With a sly grin, Kazu told him about a restaurant across town, owned by some 'friends' of his, and invited Ryan to join him. Flattered by the invite, and still unaware of the potential trouble looming around the corner, Ryan agreed. The two men left the warm glow of the ramen shop behind, disappearing into the neon-lit labyrinth towards this new, unknown destination.

A short taxi ride later, Ryan and Kazu found themselves standing outside a nondescript building in Roppongi. Before they stepped in, Kazu turned to Ryan, his previously jovial demeanor replaced by a more serious one. "You owe me a hundred US dollars for being your guide," Kazu stated matter-of-factly. The stark change in Kazu's tone and the sudden demand for payment caught Ryan off guard. He felt a surge of anger, "What? Guide? You said your friends had a good restaurant. I'm not giving you anything."

With an unsettling calmness, Kazu responded, "Welcome to the world of Yakuza, Mr. American tourist. This is how things work here. Welcome to Japan." Ryan's anger didn't subside, but a newfound fear started creeping in. Just as the confrontation was about to escalate, a police officer approached them. "Is everything okay here?" he inquired. Ryan looked at Kazu, then at the officer. "No officer. No problem at all." At this, Kazu looked at Ryan with a surprised expression, and for a moment, the tension in the air seemed to dissipate. The Police Officer nodded, looked them both over and walked away. Kazu looked at Ryan curiously, "You didn't talk. Why?" Ryan looks back at him, "I'm not a rat." Kazu is curious, "A rat?" Ryan nods. "Somebody who tells on other people." Kazu processes this. After a long pause, he nods. "Come inside. Have dinner with me." Ryan just looks at him. Kazu continues, "I have had trouble with the local Police. I owe you for not making it worse." Something in his tone was fascinating to Ryan. Just a moment ago, he was ice cold, threatening him for money. Now he was inviting him for dinner, and his offer felt kind and sincere. Kazu nods, "Serious. Dinner on me. Part of Ryan was concerned what would happen if he refused, so he nodded "yes" and they entered the restaurant.

Inside the restaurant, the tension that had previously gripped them seemed to melt away as they sat down at a low table strewn with an assortment of appetizers. Kazu ordered a round of sake as Ryan began to talk about his life back in America. "I'm here for work," Ryan explained, "I'm from California, Los Angeles. It's different from Tokyo, but there's a certain similarity in the buzz, the energy." He talked about his job, the tech industry, and his love for martial arts.

Kazu listened attentively, occasionally interjecting with perceptive comments or questions. As the sake flowed, the conversation took a lighter turn. "If you want women, or parties," Kazu offered with a roguish grin, "you just let me know. Tokyo can be fun – and if you like martial arts, I will get us some tickets. We have great MMA here in Japan."

As they finished their meal, Kazu pulled out a business card and handed it to Ryan. It was simple and elegant, with just his name and a phone number. Turning it over, Ryan found another number scribbled in pen at the back. "That's my cell," Kazu said casually. "In case you need anything. Anything at all. I will make it happen." The evening ended on a note of camaraderie and mutual respect, a far cry from the tension that had marked its beginning. As they stood up to leave, Kazu asks, "Tell me one thing?" Ryan nods, "Yeah, what's up?" Kazu looks him over, "You didn't back down earlier. Why not? You weren't scared?" Ryan grins, "I was scared, but I said fuck it. If you were going to hurt me, you were going to hurt me." Kazu nods in approval, "Like a Samurai. Or a Yakuza. I respect that." Ryan nods, "How did you get into this? Being a Yakuza?" Kazu looks deeply into his eyes. "That's a story for another night."

Ryan returned to his hotel, the glittering lights of Tokyo painting a mesmerizing backdrop to his thoughts. His encounter with Kazu stirred something within him: curiosity, excitement, and an undercurrent of danger. Stepping into his room, he felt the sharp contrast between the bustling metropolis outside and the serenity within. The room was a minimalist blend of traditional Japanese design and modern western comfort. He unpacked his suitcase, the mundane task grounding him in reality after the surreal evening. Slipping into the crisp bed linens, he stared at the ceiling, his mind replaying the night's events. The city's energy, Kazu's penetrating gaze, the subtle threats, the unexpected offer of friendship - it was something out of a movie. As he drifted into sleep, he found himself looking forward to the next chapter of his Tokyo journey, despite the looming day at the office that would start in just a matter of hours. The last thought on his mind was Kazu's parting words, promising a tale of how he fell into the Yakuza life.

Chapter Three

Boardroom Yakuza

Ryan's day began at the Tokyo Gaming home offices, a sleek modern building that was an architectural marvel with its all-glass exterior. The interior was equally impressive yet inviting, featuring comfortable carpeting that softened the industrial feel of the space. The sprawling open layout was punctuated by a maze of cubicles, each housing an employee engrossed in their work. The rhythmic tap-tap-tapping of keyboards was the only sound echoing in the vast, glass-encased office, a testament to the intense focus and dedication of the employees.

Ryan's footsteps were muffled by the thin gray carpet as he navigated his way through the office, taking in the corporate atmosphere. The dichotomy between this world and the one he had glimpsed last night was stark. While there was a certain element of adrenaline in both, the nature of the challenges and risks were worlds apart. As he took his place among the digital samurais of the 21st century, he couldn't help but feel a twinge of anticipation for the upcoming night. His thoughts were momentarily distracted by the ringing of a phone, a reminder of the corporate battlefield he was now part of. His journey in Tokyo was proving to be more complex and thrilling than he had ever anticipated.

Settling into his cubicle, Ryan began to immerse himself in his work, when a pretty, young Japanese woman in her twenties approached. She had an air of simplicity and grace about her, with her luminous dark eyes radiating warmth, and her glossy hair neatly tied back. "Hi, I'm Yumi," she said, extending a small wooden Torii gate towards him. Painted bright red with black accents, the miniature trinket was exquisite in its detailing.

"I heard you were new here, so I thought I'd get you a little house-warming gift for your cubicle," she explained, her words punctuated by a friendly smile. "It's a Torii gate, a traditional Japanese symbol for beginnings. Consider it a charm for good fortune in your new journey."

Ryan accepted the gift, the weight of the small Torii gate in his hands somehow grounding, providing a tangible link to the culture he was starting to find so intriguing. Yumi, noticing his interest in the trinket, continued, "I also work in game design. It's always nice to meet a fellow designer. Welcome to the team, Ryan."

As she walked away, Ryan couldn't help but admire how the Torii gate added a burst of color to his otherwise monotonous gray cubicle. This small token, a symbol of his new journey, was a delightful bridge between his professional life and the adventurous path he was embarking on in Tokyo. It served as a constant reminder that he was part of two worlds, each with its own challenges and rewards.

Once Yumi had disappeared from sight, Ryan redirected his attention back to his desk, his gaze focused on the large monitor in front of him. He was in the process of getting acclimated when another interruption came, this time in the form of an elegant lady in her forties, her hair wound into a sleek bun. She wore an air of sophistication and warmth in equal measure. "Hello Ryan, I'm Mariko from Human Resources," she introduced herself, extending a sleek company cell phone towards him.

"I trust you're settling in well? This here," she said, pointing to the phone in her hand, "is your company phone. While you're here in Japan, you'll need it. It has all the phone numbers and emails of everyone in the office in its directory."

Ryan accepted the phone from her, a string of thank you's leaving his lips. Mariko responded with a nod, her warm smile making the unfamiliar surroundings feel slightly more like home.

As Ryan was familiarizing himself with the new phone, a tall figure emerged from the crowd of professionals bustling about. A man in his mid-fifties, with sharp features and an aura of authority, strode towards him. His gaze was stern, and his posture radiated seriousness. He extended his hand towards Ryan, introducing himself as Jun Zushi, the head of the marketing department. "Ryan, nice to meet you. I'd like you to join us for an internal meeting in the boardroom," Jun requested, his tone leaving no room for refusal.

Ryan glanced at his watch. It was just after five in the evening, but he sensed that the long day was far from over. With a nod of agreement, he rose from his desk, leaving his newly assigned cubicle. He followed Jun through the labyrinth of desks and activity, heading towards the boardroom. Encased in elegant glass walls, the boardroom was a symbol of transparency and sophistication, mirroring the values of the company he was now a part of. He took a deep breath, preparing himself for the next chapter of his professional journey in Tokyo.

The meeting proceeded with an intensity that Ryan had seldom experienced. Jun's frustration was palpable, his eyes darting around the room as he berated his team for their lack of creativity and original thought. His words, while harsh, were not without reason. He emphasized the importance of a robust go-to-market strategy and expressed his disappointment that one had not yet been developed. "We're a creative powerhouse, are we not?" Jun challenged, his gaze piercing through each team member. "We're not here to repeat what's already been done. We need fresh, innovative ideas, and we need them fast. Sato San is not going to be pleased if we present her with the same generic strategies upon her return. I will not accept anything less." Jun's stern gaze softened slightly, his tone more encouraging than before. "I believe in the potential of this team. But I need you to step up, to bring your A-game. If you need help, ask. If you have ideas, share. I expect everyone to contribute significantly to this project." The room was silent, the tension nearly suffocating. But there was also a palpable determination. Ryan could see resolve hardening in his colleagues' eyes, a shared understanding that they all needed to do better. The meeting concluded with Jun's final words echoing in their ears, a clarion call to action that left no room for mediocrity.

As the room emptied, Ryan lingered behind for a moment, lost in thought. Jun's leadership style was strangely reminiscent of a Yakuza boss, he mused. The sharpness of his words, the intensity of his gaze, the aura of sheer intimidation that surrounded him — they all bore stark similarity to the infamous Japanese gangsters that Taka described. Jun didn't just expect respect, he demanded it. His anger was a potent tool, instilling fear in his team and compelling them to strive for excellence, not out of desire but out of necessity. No one wanted to face the wrath of an enraged Jun. It was unsettling, yes, but also oddly effective. With a final glance at the now deserted conference room, Ryan left, a newfound understanding of his boss' leadership style in mind and a renewed determination in his heart.

CHAPTER FOUR

Miles Apart

Walking out of the towering building that housed the offices, Ryan pulled out his new company-issued phone. His fingers dialed the familiar number, and he awaited the familiar voice on the other side. The phone rang, and his wife picked up.

"Hey," she greeted with a cold dispassionate tone that sent chills down his spine. His heart sunk, the warm, welcoming voice he used to know was now a frosty echo.

"Hi, I was just checking on you. How are you doing?" he asked, trying to sound cheerful.

"I'm fine. Is this a new number?" she responded with a tone that suggested otherwise.

Ryan felt a lump in his throat but continued, "Yeah, it's my new company cell. You won't believe the characters I'm meeting here. There's this guy, Kazu. He's got stories about the Yakuza that you wouldn't believe..."

"That's nice," she cut him off, her voice devoid of interest.

Ryan tried to maintain his composure, "You should see my new offices, it's..."

"Ryan, I have to go," she interrupted him again. "I'm heading to yoga."

Before Ryan could respond, the call ended. The silence was deafening. He stood there, staring at the disconnected call notification on his phone screen. A feeling of desolation wrapped around him, making him feel lower than ever. His wife's indifference felt like a punch in the gut, leaving him with an emptiness that echoed the vast, empty street he was standing on.

Staring at the abruptly ended call on his screen, Ryan felt a sharp pang of loneliness slice through him. Miles away from home, in the midst of these foreign streets, he realized the distance between him and his wife wasn't just geographical. It was emotional. A vast, cold chasm had opened up between them, one that couldn't be bridged by a simple phone call. His attempts at sharing his new experiences fell on indifferent ears. His words, once met with warmth and interest, were now unwelcome intrusions. As he pocketed his phone and continued his solitary walk, each step echoed the growing isolation that had begun to envelop him. The city's bright lights and towering buildings, once symbols of exotic opportunity, had turned into stark reminders of his solitude. His heart ached with a profound sense of loneliness, painting his new life in shades of blue.

Seeking solace in the anonymity of the city, Ryan decided to immerse himself in the local culture and headed to a traditional eatery. As he walked through the rustic doorway, the warm fragrance of home-cooked meals filled his nostrils and brought a faint smile to his face. He took a seat at a bustling corner, watching a kaleidoscope of people from all walks of life. The clatter and chatter around him drowned out his own thoughts, providing a temporary respite from the war that raged inside his heart.

As he savored the local delicacies, each bite seemed to offer a bit of comfort, a little distraction from his painful reality. Observing the interactions around him, he yearned for the time when his own conversations were brimming with joy and warmth. He dwelled on his solitude, realizing that the first step towards bridging the gap with his wife would be to understand and address his own feelings. He left the restaurant, his mind a little less burdened, his heart a little more hopeful. The city lights seemed a little less harsh, and the towering buildings a little less intimidating. With new-found resolve, he decided to confront his challenges head-on, hoping to find a way to mend the frayed edges of his marriage.

As he ventured further into the city's nightlife, Ryan found himself drawn to the faint sounds of music emanating from a small karaoke bar. He decided to step in, the festive atmosphere offering a welcome contrast to his earlier solitude. To his surprise, he spotted Mika, a colleague from work, seated with a group of women he recognized from the design team.

As he entered, Mika saw him and immediately flagged him over, inviting him to join, he was greeted with warm smiles and clinks of glasses. As the night wore on and the alcohol flowed, the conversation started veering towards their colleagues. Mika, taking the lead, began to share her observations about their CEO Megumi Sato. They all agreed that Megumi was an incredibly intelligent woman. However, they felt she was disconnected from the team. Her absence at work functions and perceived lack of a personal life led to assumptions that she was cold-hearted and peculiar. Ryan listened, sipping his drink slowly, the image of the solitary Megumi Sato adding another layer to the complex tapestry of life in his new company.

Mika continued, "Megumi Sato is brutal. Good at what she does but just a rotten person. You can work twelve hours a day and always give one hundred percent. She sees you in the hallway and just looks right through you. I cannot stand her... but, I've heard rumors...if this game launch turns out to be a failure, Jun is likely next on her list. She is going to throw him out." There were nods of agreement around the table, the air thickening with the seriousness of the revelation. Mika continues, "At least that would be a win."

Ryan thought to himself, "Well, at least I know who Sato San is now.."

"Jun is so scummy." one of the designers piped up, her words slurred slightly from the alcohol. "He's always been so political, always looking out for himself. I mean, it's no secret. He'd throw any of us under the bus to save his own skin. That's just who he is. I hope she fires him." The group muttered in agreement, their earlier mirth replaced by the sobering reality of office politics. The complexity of their work environment, with its alliances and power struggles, was a stark contrast to the vibrant, carefree ambiance of the karaoke bar.

"Hey, let's lighten things up a bit," Ryan interjected, raising his glass high. "We're here to have a good time, let's forget about work. Let's toast to us, the heart and soul of this company. To the ones who put in the long hours, who dream the big dreams. To us!" There was a chorus of cheers, and glasses clinking together, the previous tension dissipating as laughter filled the air again. The night drew on, filled with more drinks, off-key singing, and camaraderie.

As it started winding down, Mika, slightly swaying with the effects of the alcohol, sidled up to Ryan. Her eyes were sparkling, a mischievous smile on her lips. She leaned in closer, her voice dropping to a flirtatious whisper. "Ryan," she began, her fingers lightly brushing his arm. "How about we continue this party, just us, at a more private venue? Like, say... your hotel?"

Ryan was stuck. He longed for intimacy. He wanted so badly to be desired. He wanted to put his pain and loneliness behind him. He looked at Mika, her eyes filled with desire and expectation. He shook his head, "Thank you so much. I am flattered. I really am, but I'm married." She was not taking "no" for an answer. She peered deep into his eyes, "Is she here in Tokyo?" He shakes his head. She continues, "I will make you forget all about her. Trust me." Ryan takes a deep breath, "I can't. I really can't. But if I were single.." She gives him a pouty look, "You have my number. If you change your mind..?" Her offer hangs in the air. Ryan smiles tentatively, still torn with the dilemma.

With that, she kisses him sweetly on the cheek and slides back over to her friends. Ryan looks at her wistfully.

Ryan pulls out his phone and types out a text message to his wife, "Hope you enjoyed yoga. Call me later if you have some time." He hits send.

Ryan dials his wife's number once again, his heart pounding against his chest as the dial tone sounds out. "Hi, it's me," he begins, trying to keep his voice steady. He tells her about the night, the laughter, the camaraderie, carefully omitting Mika's proposition. He asks about her day, making an effort to sound interested in her yoga class, her book club meeting, anything to bring a trace of warmth to her voice. But her responses remain curt and disinterested, her tone as cold and unyielding as a winter night. "Yeah, that sounds great," he says, his voice filled with false cheerfulness. "I love you," he adds, hoping to elicit some semblance of emotion from her. But all he gets in return is a quiet "Okay, bye." before she hangs up. Sighing heavily, Ryan puts his phone away and starts the long, lonely walk back to his hotel, the city lights shimmering around him, a stark contrast to the darkness spreading in his heart.

CHAPTER FIVE

The Offer

The following morning, Ryan was hard at work in his cubicle, his focus laser-locked on the spreadsheet illuminating his screen. He was in the midst of a complicated financial analysis when a new email notification appeared. It was from Jun Zushi, his boss. The subject line read, "Need to Talk". Ryan felt a flutter of anxiety. Taking a deep breath, he clicked on the email. It asked him to come to Jun's office at his earliest convenience.

With a sense of foreboding, Ryan navigated the maze of cubicles to reach his boss's office. Jun was seated behind his desk, a stern expression on his face. As Ryan entered, Jun motioned for him to take a seat. "Ryan," Jun began, "I'll get straight to the point. We have an opening in our Tokyo office, and we'd like you to consider relocating permanently."

Ryan's eyebrows shot up in surprise. "Here? Permanently?" he repeated, the words sounding alien as they left his mouth. He was taken aback by the offer. It was a big step, a life-altering decision. He needed time to process it. "I... would need to talk it over with my wife, but thank you. I really appreciate it," he stammered, earning a nod of understanding from Jun. Jun adds, "We have significant issues here in this office. I need somebody with a fresh perspective. Somebody with drive and skill. I need you. I hope that you can make this work." He left the office, the offer weighing heavy on his mind. Would this be the change he needed, or just another complication in his already complex life?

Back at his desk, Ryan continued to chew over Jun's words when he noticed Mika approaching. Mika was holding a stack of documents in her hand. "Ryan," she started, catching her breath slightly, "Jun wants you to take a look at these before they get to him." She extended the documents in his direction. Ryan raised an eyebrow. He had only been in his current position for a few days, and already he was being pulled into matters of importance.

Mika, looking both surprised and curious, asked, "Moving up fast What's your secret?" Ryan just shook his head, shrugging lightly. "I wish I knew, Mika. I really do," he responded, his gaze falling back to the stack of paperwork that had just been added to his desk. It was clear that things were changing rapidly for Ryan, and it was just as unclear where these changes would lead. Mika gives him a seductive smile, "In case you were wondering, it wasn't the alcohol. My offer still stands." She flashes a cute smile and walks away. Ryan watches her intently as she walks away before turning intently back to his work.

As the clock on the wall struck 11 p.m., Ryan was still at the office, the last soul in a sea of deserted cubicles. His eyes were tired, but his mind was alert, attentively scribing notes onto the last sheet of the hefty document. Meticulously reading every line, every detail, he felt the weight of responsibility weighing heavily on his shoulders. As he concluded his notes, he took a small post-it note from his desk and jotted down a reminder. He peeled off the note, its neon color contrasting sharply with the white mounds of paperwork, and stuck it atop the stack. Carefully he rose, the day's fatigue hanging on his frame. With the stack of papers in his hand, he ambled over to Jun's office, its door standing ajar in the dim lighting. Setting the documents on Jun's immaculate desk, he couldn't help but feel a strange mix of exhaustion and exhilaration. He was indeed moving up fast, and the silent, empty office seemed to echo the significance of this moment.

With a heavy sigh, Ryan exited the building and hailed a taxi. The ride was silent and provided him an opportunity to gather his thoughts. His hotel room, bathed in the soft, luminescent glow of the city lights, felt both familiar and foreign. He let the weight of his body press into the plush armchair, bringing his cellphone to his ear. The ring echoed in his ear before the familiar voice of his wife answered on the other line.

"Hey, it's me," he began, his voice steady. He told her about the offer to stay long term in Tokyo. There was a pause, a silence that seemed to stretch and bend the seconds into minutes. When his wife finally responded, her voice was firm, resolute. "I think it's a good idea," she said. "But you should stay there... by yourself. I want a divorce. It's over." The words hung heavy in the air, a tangible testament to the distance that had grown between them, not just in miles, but in their hearts. Dumbfounded and at a loss for words, Ryan sat frozen. He was snapped back to reality by the sudden click on the other end of the phone line. Quickly, he re-dialed the number and it went straight to voicemail. He tried again and again for more than an hour. His fatigue was replaced by shock and a mind racing to figure out a solution. Here he sat, just like this, redialing, rehearsing the script in his head of how he would win her back. If only she would pick up. After a countless number of calls, he finally flipped a switch in his head. It was over.

CHAPTER SIX
Weekend Work

Ryan sat at his desk, engrossed in his work, when the chime of an incoming email broke his concentration. The sender: Jun, his boss. The request seemed simple, yet it carried an undertone of seriousness. He was being asked to come to Jun's office.

As Ryan walked past rows of cubicles, his mind raced. What could Jun want? His heart pounded as he knocked on the heavy wooden door of Jun's office. Jun's voice, muffled and warm, beckoned him inside. The office was immaculate, every object placed as if it had been measured for its precise location.

"Thanks for coming so quickly," Jun began, his eyes reflecting a sense of appreciation. "I wanted to talk to you about the presentation. You did an exceptional job. Thank you for getting that back to me last night." Relief washed over Ryan, and he felt a sense of accomplishment. He was being acknowledged for his hard work.

"I'd like you to present it to Megumi when she returns on Monday," Jun added, his eyes holding a hopeful glint. Ryan agreed, his mind already sorting out the details of the presentation. "And there's something else," Ryan added, taking a breath before he continued, "I've decided to stay. Permanently." Even as Ryan was telling Jun, it still felt unreal.

Jun's face broke into a wide smile, "That's excellent news, you have made me very happy. We're thrilled to have you here." Jun's words, while kind, did little to alleviate the reality Ryan would soon face. His decision to stay, coupled with the severing of his marital ties, painted a bittersweet picture of the path he had chosen. On top of it all, he would need to deliver the presentation to Megumi on Monday. This promises to be a stressful weekend.

Back in his elegant hotel room, Ryan sat hunched over a laptop, his concentration riveted on the screen. A PowerPoint presentation, filled with charts, graphs, and bullet points, shone back at him, illuminating the room with a sterile glow. The once steaming tray of room service food, now cold and half eaten, sat neglected on the corner of the sleek mahogany desk. His rehearsed words echoed in the empty room, bouncing off the bare walls and tall mirrors.

His mind fluttered back to Jun's words, "present it to Megumi..." A shudder of anticipation ran through him at the thought of the looming Monday. The click of his laptop keys became the only sound in the room, each stroke slicing through the late-night silence. A glance at the digital clock on the bedside table told him it was well past midnight - 1 a.m. to be precise. Yet sleep was a distant thought, as his mind was too full of pie charts, bar graphs, and the fragments of the life that were slowly and irreversibly slipping away.

Ryan rubbed his eyes, the harsh light of the laptop screen blurring his vision. He paused, reaching out to pick up his cell phone from the desk, the cool metallic surface a stark contrast against his warm palm. He dialed a familiar number, waiting for the dial tone to be replaced by his wife's voice. His heart pounded in his chest as he started, "Listen, I think we can work this out." His voice was steady, each word weighed heavy with anticipation and hope. He made an impassioned plea, laying out his feelings, his mistakes, and his desire to mend things.

There was a long silence on the other side of the line, before his wife finally responded. Her voice was soft, yet distant, "I will think about it, Ryan." The words hung in the air, holding a glimmer of possibility that they could, perhaps, mend their fraying ties. He hung up, placing the phone back onto the desk, the screen's glow reflecting off its polished surface. The room was once again swallowed by silence, punctuated only by the relentless ticking of the digital clock. The possibility brought a strange sense of calm, a slim ray of hope piercing through the chaos of numbers and charts that clung to his mind.

Ryan woke up early as the faint rays of morning sun pierced through the curtains. The alarm showing 5 a.m. on his digital clock, he pulled on his sneakers and stepped out into the chilly morning air. The streets were empty, and the soft echo of his footsteps against the pavement was the only sound accompanying him on his jog.

An hour later, he was back at the hotel, his body alive with the buzz of adrenaline. He took a quick shower, letting the hot water wash away the remnants of fatigue. Clad in a crisp white bathrobe, he went back to his desk. His hair still damp from the shower. The laptop screen flickered to life, the charts and graphs staring back at him.

It was Sunday, and Ryan had one more day to prepare. The stakes were high, but so was his determination. As he dove into the presentation, the numbers and graphs began to take on new meaning - they were no longer just data, but his ticket to his dream job. The next hours were spent refining every detail, every word of his presentation until he was satisfied. As the day turned into night, he felt ready, hopeful, and more determined than ever. The figures on the screen no longer daunting, but a symbol of the life he was fighting to claim.

Exhausted, yet satisfied with his progress. Ryan closed his laptop and climbed into bed. Getting some much needed sleep to prepare for Monday.

CHAPTER SEVEN
The Presentation

As Monday morning dawned, the office was a hive of activity. Ryan sat at his desk, attempting to concentrate on last-minute adjustments to his presentation, but his nervousness was palpable. His normally steady hands shook slightly as they moved swiftly across the keyboard. His heart pounded in his chest as the clock on the wall ticked closer to the meeting time.

Out of the corner of his eye, he saw Jun approaching. "Ryan, it's time. Please come to the boardroom," Jun said, his voice a mix of reassurance and anticipation. Ryan nodded, took a deep breath and pushed back his chair. Together, they navigated the bustling office and made their way toward the boardroom.

The boardroom was already populated with a handful of executives, their stern faces engrossed in scattered conversations. Ryan and Jun found their seats; the murmurs of conversation dimmed as they settled in. The room had an almost tangible air of tension and expectation.

Then, Megumi Sato walked in. She was stunningly beautiful and immaculately dressed, each piece of her attire meticulously chosen to exude an aura of both power and elegance. Her face was beautiful, a perfect blend of soft features and sharp angles, but it was devoid of any discernible emotion. Jun introduced her to Ryan, and as their eyes met, there was a spark, an inexplicable attraction. Yet, she maintained her stoic calm, her eyes revealing nothing of the emotions that might have been simmering beneath the surface.

Ryan stood, his pulse quickening, and stepped toward the front of the room. He clicked through to the first slide of his presentation, and began to speak. His voice was steady, his delivery precise. Each slide revealed more of the carefully crafted plan he and Jun had developed over days of grueling effort. As he concluded, he looked out at the executives and saw nods of agreement and supportive murmurs. There was a moment of silence before Megumi finally spoke, her voice measured and calm. "I agree with this plan. Let's move on it immediately." With that, she rose from her seat and left the room. As she reached the door, she turned back to look at Ryan. Their eyes locked, and she gave him a slight, almost imperceptible smile before disappearing down the hallway.

The tension in the room had dissipated; the remaining executives, all older Japanese men, rose from their seats. As they filed out of the room, they each gave Ryan a reassuring pat on the shoulder. Jun was the last to leave. He turned to Ryan, his face breaking into a smile of genuine pride. "You did an excellent job," he said, his tone conveying not just approval, but respect.

Ryan was on top of the world.

Back at his desk, Ryan allowed himself a moment of visible elation. His fingers drummed a triumphant rhythm on the desktop, and a smile played at the corners of his lips. As he was basking in his post-presentation glow, Mika approached, a curious expression on her face. "How did the presentation go?" she asked, her voice laced with genuine concern. Ryan looked up at her, the corners of his mouth lifting in an easy smile. "It went okay," he said, his tone casual, as if he weren't still buzzing with adrenaline.

Mika, seemingly satisfied with his response, shifted the conversation. "By the way, Hiro's celebrating his birthday tonight. We're all heading out for dinner. Want to join us?" she asked. Ryan's smile faded slightly. He appreciated the offer but wasn't ready to shift from the solitary victory of the day to a social gathering. He politely declined, "I really appreciate the invitation, Mika, but I think I'm going to take it easy tonight. Please wish Hiro a happy birthday for me." Mika nodded, a hint of disappointment in her eyes, but she respected his decision and turned to leave, leaving Ryan alone with his triumphant thoughts.

Ryan decided to celebrate his victory by treating himself to a lavish dinner at an upscale restaurant. Sitting alone at a table in the beautifully lit dining space, he savored each bite of his meal – a well-earned treat. As he concluded his dinner, he stood up and exited the restaurant, stepping out onto the bustling street.

Feeling an unexpected pang of loneliness, he reached for his phone to call his wife, only to be met with her voicemail. A sense of unease crept over him, but he shook it off, realizing that she must be busy. In a spur-of-the-moment decision, he dialed Mika's number, deciding to join Hiro's birthday celebration after all. "Mika, where are you guys?" he asked, trying to keep his voice casual, "Mind if I join you?"

CHAPTER EIGHT

Nirvana

The atmosphere at Hiro's birthday celebration was electric. The crowd in the popular nightspot Club Nirvana was a colorful blur of familiar faces, laughter echoing through the space as Ryan finally arrived. Mika spotted him first, her face lighting up with a surprised smile. "Ryan!" she exclaimed, "So happy you're here!" Ryan shrugged, grinning. "Me too. Thanks for the invite" he said, his eyes scanning the room until they landed on Hiro.

"Happy birthday, Hiro," Ryan called out, making his way towards him. Hiro turned, his face breaking into a broad smile upon seeing Ryan. "Hey, you survived Megumi. I heard you crushed it!" Hiro exclaimed, clapping Ryan on the shoulder. The camaraderie was infectious, and the initial pang of loneliness Ryan had felt was quickly replaced by a sense of warmth and belonging.

As the night wore on, the celebration transformed into a full-blown party. Colleagues became friends, barriers melted away, and for a fleeting moment, Ryan found himself in a state of nirvana. Surrounded by new friends, he felt a sense of contentment washing over him - a stark contrast to his solitary victory earlier in the day. His decision to join the party had, after all, turned his evening into an unexpected celebration of not only Hiro's birthday but also of friendships, camaraderie, and life itself.

As the pulsating music gave way to a more mellow melody, Ryan, Mika, and a few others from the group found themselves gathered around a table, drinks in hand, their conversation flowing as freely as the alcohol. Megumi's name surfaced in the chatter, drawing a chorus of reactions from the group.

Ryan hesitated for a moment before speaking up, "I think Megumi's nice, there is something about her," he said, a soft, uncharacteristic glow in his eyes as he defended her. His statement hung in the air, stirring the group into a brief silence. Mika was the first to respond, her voice laced with a hint of jealousy.

"Megumi is a bitch," She stated flatly, her tone carrying an undercurrent of bitterness, "She's mean and vindictive. No redeeming qualities." The others murmured in agreement, while Ryan simply stared into his drink, his thoughts veering towards Megumi and the enigmatic person he was feeling just under the surface of her cold exterior.

Ryan looked up from his drink, meeting Mika's gaze unflinchingly. "I think you all are being a bit harsh on her," he said, his voice calm yet firm. "Yes, she can be tough but consider the position she's in, the massive pressure she's under. She's the CEO of a multi-billion dollar company. Every decision she makes affects millions of lives. In such an environment, survival often requires adopting a certain persona. It doesn't mean she's a bad person, rather, it's just a sign of the sacrifices she has to make to keep the company growing." His words were met with silence, the group pondering over his perspective. This was a side of Ryan they hadn't seen before - empathetic, understanding, and unafraid to voice his opinions. Mika's eyes narrowed. She sensed a romantic tone to Ryan's defense of Megumi.

As the party started to wind down, Mika and Ryan found themselves standing outside, bathed in the soft glow of the streetlights. The chill in the air did little to dampen the intensity of the moment. Mika, swaying slightly, offered once more to accompany Ryan to his hotel room, "We can have a nightcap," she suggested, her voice a whisper against the quiet of the night. Ryan, however, politely declined, his mind still churning with thoughts of the earlier conversation.

Mika's gaze narrowed, a pang of jealousy gnawing at her as she studied Ryan. "You're thinking about Megumi, aren't you?" she asked, her words laced with bitterness. Before Ryan could respond, Mika continued, her voice a warning, "Megumi will only break your heart, Ryan. She doesn't care about anyone but herself." Ryan merely looked at Mika, his expression unreadable. "Be careful, Ryan," Mika whispered, her jealousy giving way to genuine concern, "Megumi is not who you think she is." Ryan just stood there, trying to process all of this.

"Why do you keep turning me down, Ryan?" Mika asked, her voice barely a whisper in the hushed silence of the night. Ryan, looking at the woman standing before him, took a deep breath, preparing to answer her question with brutal honesty. "Mika," he began, his voice steady, "I genuinely like you, I do. But work is not a place for relationships, not for me. Not for us." He paused, his expression somber, "And yes," he added, "technically, I am still married." The words hung in the air, their implications dawning on Mika. She looked at Ryan, a mix of emotions playing on her face. "Technically?," she asked. Ryan nodded, "It's really complicated.. A lot going on." A touch of sadness in his eyes. Mika senses that there is more to this as she nods, "If you need me, as a friend, I am here. Okay?" She and Ryan share a look of sincere connection. Ryan smiles at her and he kisses her on the cheek.

CHAPTER NINE

Execution

The morning sun poured in through the windows of the office, casting long shadows on the floor. Ryan was at his desk, already immersed in reports and emails, when he heard the familiar voice of Jun, his boss. "Ryan, come with me," Jun requested, the seriousness in his tone hard to miss. Ryan followed without a word.

Jun led Ryan up to the floor hosting the executive suites, an area he hadn't been to before. As they reached a polished mahogany door with the name 'Ryan McFarlane' etched on a brass nameplate, in English and Japanese Jun gestured for Ryan to enter. What greeted Ryan inside was beyond his wildest expectations.

His new office was a roomy, beautifully designed space, filled with natural light from the large windows that overlooked the city skyline. A large mahogany desk sat in the middle of the room, surrounded by plush leather armchairs. Bookshelves lined one wall, filled with books and mementos, while the other wall featured a state-of-the-art flat screen TV. Ryan was genuinely shocked, his mouth agape as he took in the sight of his new workspace.

"Welcome to your new office, Ryan," Jun announced, a hint of a smile tugging at the corners of his mouth as he watched Ryan's reaction. The enormity of the situation began to sink in, and Ryan could only muster a stunned, "Thank you, Jun. This is... beautiful." Ryan took a moment to truly appreciate his new professional journey, promising himself to rise up to the expectations that came with the new space. Jun looks into Ryan's eyes with a serious shift, "You earned this. Now you need to deliver." Ryan just realized that there would be a lot of eyes on him. The presentation was the easy part. As the U.S. Navy Seals would say, "Yesterday was the only easy day."

Engrossed in his work, Ryan sat behind his new desk, his gaze fixated on the extensive spreadsheets that crowded his desktop monitor. The hustle and bustle of activity outside his office was just a blur until a familiar figure caught his attention. Megumi, trailed by a few colleagues he had interacted with on a few occasions, breezed past. The frosty look she threw his way as she felt his eyes on her sent a chill down Ryan's spine. Her eyes were hard, devoid of the friendliness they held the day of his presentation. His heart pounded in his chest as he watched her disappear down the hallway, a foreboding sense of unease settling in. Ryan couldn't help but wonder what had caused this shift in the way she looked at him.

Lost in the intricate maze of data and numbers, Ryan barely registered the figure standing at his office doorway. It was only when Jun's voice broke through his intense concentration that he looked up, surprised. "Join me for lunch?" Jun asked, leaning casually against the door frame. A quick glance at his wristwatch made Ryan do a double-take. It was already 2 pm, the afternoon having slipped away in a cascade of work. Blinking in surprise, he nodded, pushing back from his desk as he replied, "Sure, Jun. I didn't realize how late it was. Lunch sounds perfect."

As Ryan and Jun moved towards the gleaming executive dining hall, trays stacked high with a variety of gourmet dishes, the clatter of utensils, and the hum of quiet conversations formed a backdrop to their lunchtime respite. The plush chairs, pristine tablecloths, and the view of the city skyline from the floor-to-ceiling windows created a stark contrast to the adjoining, more standard cafeteria. As they were discussing their latest project over bites of their meal, Ryan's eyes drifted towards the other dining area.

Through the glass partition, he could see Mika and a group of colleagues laughing and chatting as they joined the queue, trays in hand. The casual camaraderie of the "normal" employees, their laughter ringing out genuinely, drew a smile from Ryan. He remembered the short stint when he was one of them, free from the pressures and expectations that came with his new role.

Suddenly, he felt a pang of nostalgia mixed with a newfound understanding of his current position. The executive dining area, luxurious and exclusive, was a symbol of the responsibility now resting on his shoulders. The journey from there to here, Ryan realized, was more than just a career progression; it was a transformation that warranted new alliances, new expectations, and new realities. His gaze shifted back to Jun, now discussing the company's upcoming strategies, and he knew he had crossed an invisible line into a new realm of corporate life.

The night descended, and the bustling corporate hub fell into a quieter rhythm. The clock on the wall read 11 pm, its hands cutting through the silence in the otherwise deserted executive wing. Ryan, still immersed in a sea of spreadsheets and project timelines, blinked up at the clock, surprised by the late hour. Swiftly packing up his folders and switching off his computer, he stood up to stretch his back and prepare for the journey home.

As he exited his office, his eyes were drawn to the faint glow emanating from one of the other executive offices. Intrigued, he approached, seeing Megumi still hunched over her desk. He gave a light knock on the door, causing her to glance upwards. A serious look in her eyes, Megumi barely registered his presence. He bid her good night and she returned to her work with barely a nod of acknowledgment. The icy demeanor was a stark contrast to the friendliness she showed him the other day. As he left the premises, the stark realities of his newfound corporate life echoed in the silence of the night. Maybe Mika and her friends were right. Maybe Megumi is a bitch? Regardless, there was something to her. Something mysterious and seductive. He wanted to get to know her, he just didn't know how to break through her icy exterior.

Ryan's initiation into the mysterious world of Japanese corporate life was proving to be a stark departure from his previous experiences. The camaraderie and simplicity of his past work environment were replaced with a labyrinth of alliances, expectations, and intricate power dynamics. This new landscape was both intimidating and invigorating, providing him a reality check on what it truly meant to navigate the corporate world. Megumi, with her ice-cold demeanor and unapproachable aura, represented the epitome of this new reality. Despite her frosty attitude, Ryan found himself drawn to her aura of mystery and ambition. As he began to understand the nuances of his new role, he couldn't help but feel a sense of curiosity and intrigue towards Megumi, and the unexplored depths of his new corporate life.

CHAPTER TEN

Midnight City

Ryan tossed and turned in his hotel bed, the events of the day replaying relentlessly in his mind. His gaze fell on the glowing digits of his wristwatch, jolting him with the realization that it was already midnight. Heaving a sigh, he accepted that sleep was evading him that night. In an attempt to clear his cluttered thoughts, he decided to embrace the silent city.

He kicked off the comforter and swung his legs off the bed, reaching for the warmup suit hanging over the room's lone chair. Slipping it on, he felt the cool fabric against his skin, a sharp contrast to the stuffy atmosphere that lingered in his room. Ryan delved into his suitcase, pulling out a pair of running shoes that hadn't seen much use recently. As he laced them up, he glanced out the window, the city's midnight hues inviting him into its electric embrace. The decision to step out into the night was both a physical activity and a metaphorical journey, a chance to run towards clarity amidst the corporate chaos that was starting to consume him. Perhaps, he thought, as he exited his room and stepped into the cool night, exercise might provide the respite he needed from his swirling thoughts about Megumi and the enigmatic corporate world.

Ryan's jog took him through the heart of Shinjuku, Tokyo, a city that never slept. Its streets, bathed in neon lights, echoed with enticing whispers of nightlife. As he traversed through the district, an unexpected sight caught his attention. It was Megumi, standing outside the towering office building, waiting to be picked up.

With a quickened heartbeat, Ryan jogged over to her. "Hey, Megumi," he panted, managing to flash a small smile. Her response was a mere tilt of her head, her expression unreadable under the city's kaleidoscopic lights. As Ryan tried to engage her in conversation, her responses were curt, almost icy, leaving him feeling somewhat rebuffed.

"Long day?" he asked, trying to bridge the growing distance between them. "Yes," she replied, her gaze fixed onto the oncoming headlights of the corporate car.

The vehicle eased up to the curb, and Megumi swiftly moved to get in, leaving Ryan standing there. "See you tomorrow, Ryan," she said, her voice almost lost in the hum of the city. As the car pulled away, a shiver ran down his spine. He stood there, his breath fogging up in the cool night air, wondering what it would take to penetrate her icy façade. Despite the rebuff, he felt a renewed determination. There was more to Megumi - and this corporate world - than what met the eye, and he was resolved to uncover it.

With Megumi's parting words still echoing in his ears, Ryan picked up his pace and jogged back to his hotel, a renewed vigor coursing through his veins. The neon cityscape blurred into streaks of color as he put his thoughts into motion, the rhythmic pounding of his feet against the pavement a soothing balm to his swirling emotions.

As he entered his hotel room, the chill of the night was quickly replaced by the warm serenity of solitude. He shed his workout gear and stepped into the shower, allowing the hot water to wash away the sweat and remnants of budding desire from his brief encounter with Megumi. Each droplet was a tiny affirmation, a reminder that he was here, in the heart of Tokyo, ready to face whatever challenges awaited him.

Cleansed and feeling somewhat lighter, he slipped into the crisp hotel sheets, his body succumbing to the day's fatigue. His mind, however, was still awash with Megumi's aloof demeanor and the enigma that was the corporate world. As he stared at the muted ceiling, he made a silent promise to himself. Tomorrow, he would start afresh, chipping away at the icy façade, one day at a time.

With this thought securely nestled in his mind, sleep quickly claimed him, pulling him into a world of dreams where the lines between reality and possibility blurred into one. As he drifted off to sleep, he had one hope - that he would find Megumi in his dreams and he would get to know her.

CHAPTER ELEVEN

Dreamscape

In the depths of slumber, Ryan's mind crafted an exquisite dreamscape, a realm far removed from the austere corporate halls he had come to associate with Tokyo. He found himself in the plush embrace of a hostess club, ensconced in an opulent booth and bathed in the warm, golden glow of strategically placed lighting. The hum of soft jazz filled the air, muted conversations punctuating the melodious rhythm.

Across from him sat a radiant Japanese woman, her luminescent allure only surpassed by the mellifluous cadence of her voice. They conversed, their topics meandering through an array of subjects, but nothing held Ryan's attention. His gaze drifted upwards, and there she was, Megumi, standing at the edge of their booth, smiling down at him. She was a vision, clad in a scintillating evening gown that mirrored the night sky, shimmering and endless.

As if on cue, the other hostess delicately extracted herself from their conversation and departed, leaving Megumi to glide gracefully into the vacated seat. For a fleeting moment, it was as if they existed outside of time, their worlds converging in this imagined reality. Ryan took Megumi's hand and delicately kissed it. She peered into his eyes, a look of desire and true connection. Ryan's heart fluttered with desire and connection.

However, the dream was short-lived. As the first rays of dawn pierced through the hotel room curtains, Ryan stirred from his sleep. He woke up with his heart pounding, his mind racing, the image of Megumi in his dreams still vivid. It was a dream, but the emotions it stirred were undeniably real.

CHAPTER TWELVE

Advice from the Yakuza

It was a typical Friday for Ryan, his focus unwavering as he navigated through the complexities of his work. The characteristic hum of activity echoed throughout the office, melding with the rhythmic tapping of his fingers on the keyboard. His workspace was a whirlwind of documents, spreadsheets, and project plans, each inch of progress met with the satisfaction of tasks getting accomplished.

Amidst this whirlpool of productivity, a knock on the door jolted Ryan from his concentration. It was Jun, his enigmatic colleague, his visage as inscrutable as ever. He stood at the doorway, a cordial smile gracing his features "Ryan," he started, "Would you care to join me for lunch?"

Ryan accepted the invitation, setting aside his work for a brief respite. They ventured together to the executive lunchroom, a space that hummed with the subtle energy of corporate camaraderie and echoed with the clink of cutlery against porcelain.

As they settled into their seats, Jun began to share his plans for the upcoming weekend. "Ryan, I'm taking my wife and our two little girls on a trip to Hakone," he said, a trace of excitement lingering in his voice. "We're planning to visit the hot springs there. The city is famous for its therapeutic waters, and the girls are absolutely thrilled."

Ryan listened, his attention piqued by Jun's recount of his family-oriented plans. There was a palpable warmth in Jun's descriptions, the familial bond evident in his words. When asked about his own plans, Ryan sighed lightly, a wry smile on his lips. "I'll be working, Jun," he replied. "There's a lot to be done, and I'd rather get ahead while I can." Jun nods his head, impressed by Ryan's dedication.

Jun, noticing the hint of resignation in Ryan's voice, decided to change the topic. "Ryan," he began, a thoughtful look in his eyes, "Have you ever had a chance to explore some of the other cities in Japan?" Ryan shook his head and replied, "No, not really. I've mostly been occupied with work." Jun smiled knowingly, understanding Ryan's commitment. Leaning back in his chair, Jun recommended, "You should definitely explore Kyoto and Osaka when you get the chance. Kyoto with its historic temples and beautiful cherry blossoms is a sight to behold. And Osaka, with its vibrant nightlife and delectable street food, is truly a gastronome's paradise." Both are perfect for weekend getaways. Ryan nods. His thoughts drifting back to Megumi.

Ryan, his thoughts still lingering on Megumi, decided to ask Jun more about her. "What about Megumi? What is her story?" He ventured, his expression thoughtful. Jun, surprised by the sudden question about their CEO, took a moment before responding, "No idea. All I know is that she loves art galleries." Ryan is curious, "Art galleries?" Jun nods, "Other than that, she is a black box." Ryan is puzzled, and Jun continues, "No idea, all I know is that she disappears every Friday afternoon, saying that she is going to visit various art exhibits." Ryan just nods. Jun's eyes narrow a bit, "Why the curiosity about Sato-san?" Ryan takes a deep breath, "Just curious, that's all." Jun just nods, trying to figure out Ryan's real intentions, "She's not very open about her life. I heard she has a brother, in Osaka I think.."

Ryan was at his desk, deeply engrossed in his work when he glanced at the time. It was 4 pm. As he looked up, he noticed Megumi gathering her belongings, preparing to leave her office. Without a second thought, Ryan stood up and walked over to his door. He looked at her and with a warm smile wished, "Have a good weekend, Megumi." She paused, meeting his gaze. A trace of a smile graced her lips as she responded, "Thank you, Ryan." With that, she turned and left the office, leaving him standing alone in the silence of the room, her words hanging in the air.

Ryan returned to his desk, his mind humming with the mystery of Megumi. Hours of work stretched out in front of him, reports and data filling the solitude of his office. He lost himself in the rhythmic dance of numbers and formulas, his screen painting his face in a cold, blue light. The clock on his computer blinked, announcing it was 7 pm.

Ryan took a deep breath, stretched out and glanced at his phone. He picked it up and typed out a quick text, "Hey, finished work. Heading home now." He hit send, the message disappearing into the ether. He started packing his belongings into his bag. Files, a water bottle, and his laptop found their way into his bag as he prepared for his nightly commute. With a final glance around his now dark office, he turned off the light and made his way out, leaving behind the silence and the intrigue of another day at the office.

Ryan made his way into the small, dimly lit restaurant tucked away in a quiet corner of the city. The rich aroma of simmering broths wafted through the air, a comforting reminder of the familiar. He was greeted by his new friend Taka, the local Yakuza who was foe turned friend, a man of significant stature, with intense eyes that hinted at a life lived on the edge. Taka smiled warmly, the lines around his eyes deepening as he did so. Yet, he maintained his hardened exterior, his cool demeanor an unmistakable echo of his local Yakuza image. They found a table in the corner, away from the prying eyes of other patrons. Ryan settled into his chair, a sigh of relief escaping him as he took in the familiar environment. They each ordered a beer, the frothy beverages arriving swiftly, a testament to the efficient service of the establishment. As he took a sip, he glanced at Taka, his mind buzzing with questions and the evening stretching out before them.

"How is work?" Taka asked, breaking the comfortable silence that had settled between them. His voice was low and calm, a soothing presence amidst the humdrum of the restaurant.

Ryan leaned back, a smile slowly spreading across his face. "Work is great, Taka. It's been keeping me on my toes, but in a good way," he admitted, his eyes reflecting a newfound contentment. He paused for a moment, taking another sip of his beer, before turning his gaze back to Taka. "You know what?" he began, "I think I've made up my mind. I've decided to stay in Tokyo permanently." His announcement hung in the air, a testament to the surprising, yet satisfying turn his life had taken in this sprawling city. Taka raises his eyebrows. Ryan asks with a sly grin, "How's your work?" Taka takes a pack of cigarettes out of his jacket and offers one to Ryan. Ryan contemplates for a moment and accepts. Taka pulls his lighter from his pocket and starts to light Ryan's cigarette before lighting his own. "That's a big thing you know?" Ryan is curious and Taka continues, "The person with the higher status always has the other person light it for them." Ryan is confused, "I just did you an honor. If you are going to stay in Japan, you need to learn these things." Taka adds. Ryan nods, "I'll get yours next time. I just need to get a new lighter." Taka grins, "And the lighter matters, not some plastic one from the local convenience store. Has to at least be a Zippo. Mine is Cartier." He shows Ryan, it's a gold Cartier. Ryan nods, "That's good to know. I'll get a good one." They grin at each other. The server comes over, takes their orders and leaves the table.

Taka takes a deep drag off of his cigarette and leans back in his chair, surveying the room, "So work is good? Any cute girls in your company?" Ryan grins, "Nah." Taka continues, "Big gaming company. In Tokyo? Yeah, there are some." Ryan chuckles, "I'll take you to the office sometime, let you see for yourself." Taka chuckles. Ryan shifts the conversation, "Your work, how is that going?" Taka takes a deep breath, "Just like yours. Busy."

Their food arrives. It's a beautiful plate of thinly sliced steak cooked to perfection. They both dig in.

Outside, the city streets of Tokyo are bustling with activity on this beautiful Friday night.

Taka and Ryan have finished eating. Multiple beer bottles set atop the table. Taka pulls the pack of cigarettes from his jacket and Ryan readily accepts. As Taka puts the cigarette in his mouth and pulls out his lighter, Ryan reaches across the table to grab the lighter, "Allow me." Taka hands Ryan the lighter and Ryan casually lights Taka's cigarette before lighting his own. Taka rests back in his chair, taking a deep drag on the cigarette. "Very good. You're learning." Ryan smiles proudly.

Just then, Taka's eyes fixate on somebody just entering the restaurant. The man, just entering, locks eyes with Taka and turns to abruptly leave. Taka stands up quickly and looks to Ryan, "Wait here." Ryan is both surprised and confused, the beers have taken their toll on him, "What's up?" Taka shoots Ryan a serious look, "Stay here. This is MY work." Ryan sits, stunned as Taka makes his way to the door.

Moments later, Ryan exits the restaurant to look for Taka. He does not have to look long. Taka punches the man. Hard. Twice in the stomach and once in the face. The man collapses. Taka looks over to Ryan calmly, "Go order us another round." Ryan stands looking at Taka, still shocked. Taka casually kneels over the fallen man and reaches into his jacket pocket. He removes the man's wallet, empties it of cash and drops the wallet on the ground next to him.

Taka walks over to Ryan, who is still standing at the door to the restaurant. He gives Ryan a grin, "Come on, let's go back in. Dinner is on him." Ryan, speechless, follows Taka back in to the restaurant.

Ryan and Taka are back at the table. Taka sits calmly as Ryan tries to process this, "So that's work huh?" Taka grins, "Just like you, I work long hours."

More hours pass and more big bottles of beer have been consumed. Ryan is visibly intoxicated, "When you asked earlier.. if there were any cute girls in my office? Taka nods and listens. Ryan continues, "There is one. She won't even talk with me. But there is something about her." Taka contemplates, "You're what, six foot three?" Ryan nods, "Six two." Taka continues, "Good looking, smart, American guy. She'll talk to you. Trust me." Ryan takes another sip of beer, "She's my CEO." Taka grins, "She's Japanese?" Ryan nods. Taka asks, "Married?" Ryan raises his eyebrows, "No idea. Nobody seems to know anything about her."

The server approaches with another round of beers. Ryan looks up appreciatively. Taka does not even acknowledge the pretty young woman.

Taka continues, "Why bother with her? This city is full of women who would want you." Ryan again raises his eyebrows, "I don't know man. I really don't know. There is just something about her."

Taka contemplates, "If she is married, drop it. If she is single, take her." Ryan laughs, "Take her? She's not a bicycle." Taka turns serious, "In Japan, women only respect strong guys. That's the attitude you need to have."

Ryan raises his glass to Taka, "Kampai, I appreciate you Taka. Just don't beat the shit out of me." Taka is unfazed by Ryan's joke, "You have what a Japanese woman would want. That guy outside? He got scared, he tried to run. Not you. When I first met you, you looked me dead in the eye. You could have told the cops on me, but you didn't. You were ready to accept whatever happened. You're a warrior."

The conversation just turned serious. Ryan's speech slightly slurred, "But she's my CEO?" Taka shakes his head, "Makes no difference. Unless she's married." Ryan nods.

Taka looks around, "Let's go. Let's get you some girls to take your mind off of your CEO girlfriend. I know a place."

Just thinking of Megumi as his girlfriend makes Ryan's heart flutter a bit. There was no other woman on earth that could take his mind off of Megumi. Ryan, in that moment was determined to win her heart. Ryan looks to Taka, "Thanks man, I'm just going back to the hotel and get some sleep."

Taka nods, "Suit yourself Ryan-san. It was good to see you."

CHAPTER THIRTEEN
Weekend Work

Saturday morning found Ryan making his way through the quiet streets of Tokyo, the city still in slumber. As he approached the towering edifice of Tokyo Gaming, the stark contrast of the deserted offices to the usual buzzing workspace felt eerily surreal. It was a day when most of the city was snuggled warmly within their homes, reveling in the tranquility of the weekend.

Ryan, however, had a different plan. His goal was singular - Megumi. And he was ready to do whatever it took, even if it meant working through the weekend. As he stepped into the empty office building, the silence echoed around him. He made his way towards the elevators, their doors sliding open with a mechanical hum that seemed to fill the void.

Upon reaching his floor, he walked across the expanse of the deserted workspace, each footstep reverberating in the silence. The sight of his own office, usually a hub of chaos and creativity, now felt like stepping into a different realm. His desk, laden with designs and reports, awaited him. Ryan had the whole office, and the whole weekend, to himself. It was time to get to work.

Hours passed in a blur as Ryan poured his heart into his work. His casual attire had become even more relaxed, shoes cast aside as he stood, socks against the plush carpet, at the whiteboard that spanned an entire wall of his office. His hand was a blur, the marker squeaking as it danced across the glossy surface, translating his thoughts into a maze of lines and diagrams. His brow furrowed in concentration, his gaze never wavering from the board. The office was quiet, save for the rhythmic sound of the marker and the soft hum of the overhead lights. This was Ryan's world, his domain where he crafted his dreams into reality, one stroke at a time.

Suddenly, Ryan's cell phone began to ring. He walks over, picks it up and notices that it is a call from Allie. He answers. He listens for a moment, "Okay, if divorce is what you want, then I am good with it too." He hangs up the phone and goes back to work.

Ryan continued to work, his eyes straining against the harsh glare of the overhead lights. His hands moved slower now, dragging the marker across the whiteboard with an effort that was becoming increasingly difficult to sustain. He paused, rubbing his eyes and stretching his aching muscles. Glancing at his wristwatch, the glowing digits read 11 pm. It was time to call it a night.

He gathered his scattered papers, neatly stacking them in his bag before switching off the lights in his office. As he stepped out into the corridor, his gaze was drawn to Megumi's office. Switching on the lights, he was met with an austere sight. The office was meticulously tidy, with no photos or personal memorabilia adorning the space. Ryan idly wondered about the woman who spent her days in this sanitized environment, devoid of any personal touches. With a final glance around the room, he turned off the lights and headed home, his mind filled with thoughts that strayed far from the drawings and reports that waited for him in his bag.

CHAPTER FOURTEEN

Thank God It's Monday

Monday morning arrived with the promise of a new beginning. Ryan, although still adjusting to the recent changes in his life, found solace in the familiar rhythm of his work. As he walked through the hallway of the office building, he ran into Jun.

"Good morning, Jun," Ryan greeted, his hand extended for a friendly shake. Jun, ever the early bird, returned the greeting with a warm smile. Ryan took a moment to update Jun on the progress they had made over the weekend. Jun listened attentively, nodding in approval as Ryan delineated the details of their advancements.

"That's fantastic, Ryan," Jun exclaimed, visibly pleased, "I knew you could do it. We are right on track!"

Ryan nodded, feeling a sense of accomplishment wash over him. He was glad that his hard work was paying off and that their project was moving forward as planned. Jun, still brimming with relief, turned to Ryan and said, "Now that we're ready, I will let Megumi know that it's time to proceed to the next stage."

"I could let her know," Ryan asks, already planning his conversation with Megumi in his head. This was the progress they had all been pushing for - the breakthrough they needed. For the first time in a while, Ryan felt truly optimistic about the days to come. The feeling of dread that usually came with Monday mornings had been replaced by a sense of anticipation. Yes, it was indeed a good Monday. June nods, "That would be great. Please let her know and cc me on the email."

Back at his desk, Ryan began composing an email to Megumi Sato. His fingers danced over the keyboard as he conveyed the good news. "Dear Megumi," he began, "I'm pleased to let you know that our progress has been faster than expected. We are ready to move forward with the next step of the execution of the plan." He briefly outlined the details, ensuring she was up-to-date with their advancements. With Jun cc'd on the email, he hit send and leaned back in his chair. He was tired, the day having taken a toll on him. Yet, the fatigue seemed insignificant when contrasted with the excitement that came from the big win. This momentum, he thought to himself, was just what the team needed to drive the project to completion.

Later in the day, the office was humming with quiet conversations and the clatter of keyboards. Ryan, refreshed from a short break, was making his way back to his office when he passed the board room. Through the glass walls, he saw Megumi standing at the head of the long, polished table, commanding the attention of a handful of executives. Her voice, strong and confident, echoed throughout the spacious room, punctuated by the occasional nods from the listeners. Ryan paused for a moment, observing from a distance. There was something about her. Something powerful, yet gentle. Closed off, yet seductive. As he watched, he was drawn to her eyes. He could not look away.

Almost as if on cue, Megumi Sato looked up and locked eyes with Ryan. She motioned Ryan into the spacious board room. Ryan's heart skipped a beat. He stood frozen for a moment before heeding her call. He enters the board room and Megumi asked him to take a seat.

A few of the execs looked over at Ryan - a mix of disdain and distrust in their eyes. Who was this guy coming in and shaking things up? A foreigner nonetheless. Megumi kicked it off by thanking Ryan for his quick turnaround on the project. Ryan nodded humbly.

Megumi continued with the meeting, calling out the urgency to regain momentum. With a strong closing statement, she ends the meeting. The room disperses quickly. Ryan hangs behind and approaches Megumi, "Thanks for the callout. I really appreciate it." She looks up from her papers that are on the table in front of her. Ryan continues, "There were a couple of points in my plan that I would love your feedback on if you have some time?" She looks back down to her papers, "I'm free tonight at seven, if you are still in the office?" Ryan tries to contain his excitement, "Yes, definitely. I will be here. Please let me know if anything comes up and you can't make it." She musters a forced smile, "Thank you, I will."

Ryan is on top of the world as he makes his way back to his office. He was feeling the fatigue of the long, work-filled weekend. Now, all he can think of is his face-to-face meeting with Megumi.

The sun has set outside of the office and the night lights of Tokyo, Japan were on full display. It's after work, and commuters and tourists alike course through the city like blood flowing through veins.

Inside of Ryan's office, he looks expectedly up at the clock on the wall. The clock strikes 7 o'clock. Ryan gets up from his desk, fixes his collar and nervously picks up a stack of papers from his desk. He makes his way out of the door and into the hallway.

He glances over at Megumi's office. The light is still on. He makes his way over, a mix of excitement, expectation and anxiety washing over him. He knocks on the door, opens it slightly and looks in. His look turns from expectation to confusion. Jun is sitting in one of the chairs aside Megumi's desk. He looks up, sees Ryan, "Come on in. Sato-san told me that you had some questions for her about the plan?" Ryan nods, "Yeah, sure. Is Sato-san going to.. join us?"

Jun shakes his head, "Uh, no. She asked me to take a look and go over it with you."

Ryan's plan has backfired. Reluctantly, he sits down, and flips open the printed material.

Ryan's meeting with Jun has ended and he makes his way back to his office. Sitting down, he takes a deep breath. Disappointment washes over him like a wave.

It has been a long day. The emotional roller coaster has taken its toll. It is time to go home. Ryan packs up his belongings and heads for the door.

CHAPTER FIFTEEN
Moving Day

Ryan steps out of the elevator into the modern elegance of his new apartment building in Tokyo's upscale Nishi Azabu neighborhood. Keys jingle in his hand as he unlocks the door to his new home. Stepping inside, he is greeted by the expansive space; a stark contrast to his previous cramped quarters.

Floor-to-ceiling windows offer sweeping views of Tokyo's skyline, the city lights twinkling like a sea of stars. He drifts from room to room, his footsteps echoing eerily off the hardwood floors and high ceilings. He stops in the kitchen, a culinary dream with its sleek, stainless steel appliances and marble countertops.

Despite the luxury, a pang of loneliness strikes him. The space seems too vast for one person, filled with silence rather than the laughter and warmth of shared memories. He looks around, the excitement of the move fading into the realization of his solitude. Each room was a canvas of potential, yet the emptiness seemed daunting. Strangely, the hotel had felt like home. Now, in his new apartment, he was truly starting over.

Ryan moves to the window, his reflection staring back at him amidst the city lights. His new life in Nishi Azabu had just begun, but with it came the stark reminder of the distance between his past and his present. The city bustled below him, yet he'd never felt so alone.

He sighs, the weight of the day settling on his shoulders. "It's just the first day," he murmurs to himself, "just the first day." His words echo back at him, a reminder that this was now his reality. The apartment, as beautiful and luxurious as it was, felt more like a gilded cage, and the city outside, as much as it was a breathtaking view, only seemed to magnify his solitude.

Ryan checks his watch and calculates the time difference in his head. He picks up the cell phone, dials a number and waits. On the other end, Allie answers, "Hello?" Ryan takes a deep breath, "Allie, it's me." Her tone softens, "You okay? You sound.. off?" Ryan makes his way over and sits on the overstuffed leather couch.

More than 30 minutes have passed. Allie continues, "It's not just one thing. Our life was .. boring. I need something more. You're just so.. safe... and predictable." Ryan nods his head to himself. He wipes a tear away from his eye, "Okay. I understand. I'll talk with work and see when I can get off. I'll come back to the U.S. and we can sign the papers. Just let me know when they are ready."

He hangs up the phone. Visibly sad, he sits in contemplation.

Chapter Sixteen

Shadow World

Ryan sits in his office, the hum of city life echoing from the streets below. The clock ticks towards five, its steady rhythm an unwelcome reminder of the home he left behind. The week had been a long one, filled with meetings, presentations, and paperwork that seemed to take him further from his past life with every signature, every nod of approval.

His office is the epitome of modern Japanese design, sleek and minimalist, but it feels cold and impersonal, a stark contrast to the cluttered, lived-in office he'd left behind in the States. He misses the photos of family and friends that used to litter his desk, the familiar coffee stain on his old paperwork, the comfortable chaos of his previous life.

The clock strikes five. He'd had enough. He packs up his laptop, switches off the monitor, and takes a last look around the office before heading for the door. The promise of dinner and a drink lured him out into the city that was still so foreign to him. As he steps out of the building and merges with the bustling crowd, he couldn't help but feel a pang of nostalgia for his old life, a life which now seemed like it belonged to another world. His gaze catches his reflection in a shop window - it's him, yet it's not. He's a shadow amidst the bright lights of Tokyo, a man caught between his past and his future.

Ryan found himself at an upscale restaurant, a place where dimly lit lanterns cast a warm glow on polished wooden tables. All around him, couples laughed and chatted in hushed tones, their closeness a stark contrast to his solitude. He watched them from the corner of his eye, his heart aching with a mix of longing and melancholy. Every laugh, every shared glance, every clink of glasses served as a painful reminder of his solitude in this buzzing city.

As he savored the last of his meal, an exquisite dish cooked to perfection, Ryan found himself adrift in thought, lost in the cacophony of the restaurant and the memories of his life that seemed a world away. He paid his bill and thanked the waiter, his words swallowed by the steady hum of conversations around him.

Stepping out into the crowded streets of Tokyo, Ryan was immediately swept up in the Friday night frenzy. Neon lights flashed in every corner, their gaudy colors reflected in the myriad of faces that passed him by. The air was filled with the tantalizing aromas of street food, the laughter of party-goers, and the constant chatter of a city that never sleeps. But amidst the crowd and the noise, Ryan felt an overwhelming sense of loneliness. He was a stranger in a familiar land, a shadow adrift in the lights of Tokyo. Ryan made a decision. Tonight, he would not be alone.

Ryan makes his way through the crowded streets. A large neon sign in purple and white catches his eye. The name "Shadow Verse" piques his interest. On the marquis, there are images of beautiful Japanese women in various stages of undress. Tonight, this was exactly what he needs.

He makes his way to the door, pays his cover charge and enters. As he makes his way inside, it was like stepping into a completely different world. It has been more than ten years since Ryan has entered a strip club. That night, he was in Los Angeles and he was with friends from college. That night, he found the whole experience depressing. That night, the dancers felt desperate and the atmosphere seedy. This however, was the complete opposite.

As he steps further into the 'Shadow Verse', Ryan is immediately struck by the elegance and opulence of the club. The plush velvet chairs and dimly lit chandeliers lend the room an air of sophistication, a stark contrast to his previous experiences. The floor is peppered with small round tables, each featuring a single, glowing, crystal lamp that casts a soothing light around the area. The walls are adorned with tasteful artwork, and a stage in the center glistens under soft lighting.

The dancers, a group of stunning Japanese women, move with a grace and rhythm that seems to mesmerize the room. They're wearing only thong bottoms and mardi gras style masks, adding an element of intrigue and mystery to their performance. Their bodies sway with a hypnotic rhythm, each movement executed with an artistic finesse that blurs the line between dance and poetry. Their masks, adorned with feathers and jewels, veil their identities but not their allure. Each dancer is a captivating performance artist, commanding attention and respect in this enclave of Tokyo's nightlife.

Without missing a beat, Ryan navigates his way through the room, settling on a plush, velvet chair that offers a good view of the mesmerizing spectacle on stage. A server, fully dressed in a tasteful and traditional Japanese outfit, approaches him. She is a young woman in her twenties, her face radiating a polite and professional warmth. Ryan places his order for a whisky on the rocks - a simple but classic choice.

In no time, the server returns with his drink, served in a beautifully etched glass that catches the dim light in a fascinating play of shadows. Ryan murmurs his thanks and takes in the alluring aroma of the whisky before taking a careful sip. The rich, smoky flavor floods his palate, lend-ing a pleasing contrast to the ethereal ballet unfolding on the stage. As he savors his drink, Ryan's gaze is locked on the dancers, their movements painting a captivating story against the soft glow of the stage lights. Each move, every subtle sway, is a testament to their skill and artistry, further enhancing the entrancing ambience of the 'Shadow Verse'.

Ryan's attention is inexorably drawn to one dancer in particular. Her movements are imbued with an undeniable sensuality, yet she carries herself with an elegance and refinement that sets her apart. The strength and grace of her dance hold a compelling allure, each calculated step a harmony of seduction and sophistication. She's a paradox, an enigma of sorts, a siren wrapped in silk and mystery.

His eyes, mesmerized, track her every motion, tracing the fluidity of her dance as it seamlessly transitions from sultry sways to poised pirouettes. He's captivated, entranced by the artistic dexterity manifest in her performance. The world around him fades into insignificance, the performers, audience, and even his whisky momentarily forgotten. All that exists is the captivating spectacle of her dance.

Then, as if responding to an unspoken cue, she breaks away from the synchronized tableau of dancers. Gracefully, almost like a gazelle, she descends from the stage and begins to weave her way through the crowd in the darkened lounge. With each step she takes towards Ryan, the palpable tension, the electric anticipation, heightens. The room seems to hold its breath as this elegant mystery makes her approach, a captivating dance of attraction that has only just begun.

She passes by Ryan and his heart drops. Just then, the touch of a silky finger caresses the side of his cheek before moving on to his neck.

As the silken finger dances up his neck, Ryan feels the pressure linger, a tantalizing touch that sends chills skittering down his spine. Then, as if in slow motion, the mysterious dancer gracefully eases onto his lap. His breath hitches, caught between surprise and anticipation. The dancer lowers her head, the shimmering mask coming tantalizingly close, revealing the eyes that he had seen only briefly, in meetings at the office - however, they were unmistakable to him. Those were the eyes of Megumi Sato, his enigmatic CEO.

The realization hits him hard, and as if feeling his shocked stillness, she halts and looks at him. Recognition flares in her eyes as she realizes that the man beneath her is Ryan, her dedicated employee. The world seems to stop spinning and music fades away as they both lock eyes, frozen in a moment of unexpected intimacy. The silence between them is deafening, charged with a plethora of unspoken words and stifled emotions.

Just as suddenly as she had come, she slips away from his lap, her movements swift and fluid. Like a wisp of smoke, she seamlessly fades into the shadows of the backstage area, leaving a stunned Ryan in her wake. His eyes, still wide with surprise, follow her retreating figure until it disappears completely, swallowed by the welcoming darkness. Although this brief encounter lasted mere seconds, it was the most passionate experience Ryan has ever experienced.

A mixture of desire, shock and confusion wash over Ryan. The only thing that he knows is that life will never be the same. He is certain of that.

CHAPTER SEVENTEEN
Alone

Back in her luxury penthouse, Megumi paces restlessly, her mind whirling with a thousand thoughts. She is dressed in her usual elegant attire, a stark contrast to the exotic ensemble she was in earlier. The sprawling living room, adorned with tasteful art pieces and plush furnishings, feels oddly oppressive tonight. The panoramic view of the city, which typically soothes her, only adds to her unrest. The glittering lights seem to mock her secret, blaring it out loud.

Her heart hammers in her chest as she thinks of Ryan, his stunned face imprinted in her mind. She recalls their chance encounter. The fear of him revealing her secret makes her stomach churn. She's always been composed and in control, but tonight, she is a tumult of emotions.

She glances at her reflection in the floor-to-ceiling mirror, her eyes betraying her anxiety. What if he tells their colleagues about her secret life? What if this revelation ruins her hard-earned reputation? Her thoughts spiral, but amidst it all, she finds an odd sense of relief. Sharing her secret with Ryan, as unintentional as it was, has unburdened her.

The realization surprises her, but she pushes it aside. Tonight, she must find a way to ensure her secret stays hidden. Tomorrow, she will face Ryan, and whatever that conversation brings, she will confront it head-on. The Megumi Sato he met tonight was vulnerable and exposed, but the Megumi he'll meet tomorrow will be as unassailable as ever. This is a promise she makes to herself as she stares out into the night, alone in her penthouse.

Overwhelmed by her thoughts, Megumi suddenly finds herself gripped by a sense of urgency. She can't wait until tomorrow, she needs to clear the air, to see him, tonight. Her hand flutters over the sleek surface of her cell phone, her heart pounding with a mix of dread and anticipation. She scrolls through her contacts list until she finds his name. Ryan. Her finger hovers for a moment over the screen, then she takes a deep, steadying breath and presses 'call'. As the phone begins to ring, she clenches her other hand into a fist, bracing herself for the conversation to come. She'd always been the one in control, and tonight would be no different. She was Megumi Sato, after all, and she would handle this, as she had handled everything else - with poise and resolve.

On the other end of the line, Ryan picks up, his voice warm and slightly groggy. "Megumi?" he asks, confusion seeping into his tone. "Is everything alright?"

With a cold, measured voice, she replies, "We need to talk. Meet me at the Katsu Grill in Shibuya in half an hour." There is no room for argument in her voice, a tone that brooks no disagreement.

There's a pause on the other end. She imagines him, sleep-ruffled and surprised, as he processes her words. Then, quite simply, he agrees. "Okay, I'll be there."

With that, she ends the call, her decision made. Whatever comes next, Megumi Sato is ready to face it.

CHAPTER EIGHTEEN
Katsu Grill

The Katsu Grill in Shibuya stood out like an oasis of light in the otherwise dark and quiet street. The restaurant was near its closing time, and the usually bustling establishment was nearly deserted. Ryan, hair still tousled from sleep, walked in. His face was instantly recognized by the hostess - a young woman with a polite smile and eyes that sparkled with curiosity. She gave him a slight bow, murmuring a respectful, "Good evening."

"I am here to meet someone," Ryan requested, his voice betraying a hint of apprehension.

The hostess nodded, leading him past the nearly empty tables, to the private room at the back. She slid open the door to reveal a dimly lit room, its minimalist style offering a stark contrast to the warm and busy main dining area. In the center of the room, under the low hanging lights, sat Megumi. Her silhouette was outlined by the dim light, making her appear both formidable and impossibly distant. Her gaze was fixed outside the window, her expression unreadable.

The hostess excused herself, leaving the two alone. Ryan took a deep breath, steeling himself for the conversation to come. He did not know what to expect, but he knew one thing - no matter what happened, it would change everything between them.

The air in the room was thick with the unspoken words and unresolved issues between Megumi and Ryan. The silence was heavy, almost tangible, and it filled the room like a tangible entity, making the space between them seem like an insurmountable barrier. Ryan glanced at Megumi, her face bathed in the soft glow of the overhead lights, her eyes still not meeting his. The usual lively spark in her eyes was replaced by a stony resolve that made his heart sink. He swallowed down the lump in his throat, the anticipation of the impending conversation causing an uneasy churning in his stomach. On the other hand, Megumi maintained her stoic charade, her gaze fixed on a point somewhere outside the window. However, her tightly clasped hands, resting on the table, betrayed her seemingly calm exterior. The tension was palpable, underscoring the gravity of the conversation they were about to have, and the potential consequences it might have on their relationship.

Megumi turned to face Ryan with a cold and expressionless look, "Please, have a seat." Ryan nods, "If this is about tonight?" She holds up her hand, cutting him off. They both sit down. Instantly she proceeds, "You saw something tonight that you shouldn't have seen. If you ever utter one word of this, you will regret it." Her words, delivered with the precision of a Katana, hang in the air. Ryan nods solemnly. She continues, "Do we have an understanding?" Ryan nods. Megumi is not convinced, "If you do share this with anyone, not only will you be removed from the company, you will..." Ryan interjects, "Your personal life is your personal life. I would never betray that." Megumi nods. He stoic exterior not reflecting the wave of relief washing over her. Ryan's words, although few, ring true to her. She feels an innate sense of trust for him. Still calm and in control she adds, "That's all. Apologies for calling you here on short notice." It is clear to Ryan that she is finished. He nods solemnly before standing. He makes his way over to the door to the private room before turning back, "Can I ask you one thing?" She nods, and Ryan continues, "I felt something tonight when you looked into my eyes. Did you feel it too?" She shakes her head, "No. I didn't." He could tell that this was a lie. Deep down, she knew it was a lie too.

Without another word, Ryan nodded and left the room. Megumi sat in quiet contemplation. Her heart was swirling with mixed emotions. She didn't want him to leave, but she forced him to. She had to. Her professional survival depended on it.

Outside the restaurant, Ryan was walking back to the train station. Deep down, he knew that she felt that spark, that wave of emotion, so raw and powerful. He made a silent vow to himself that he would find a way into her heart. No matter what. He actually chuckled to himself. This was a pretty unconventional first date.

CHAPTER NINETEEN
Prep

The morning sun poured through the windows of the bookstore, casting a warm glow on the rows of books neatly arranged. Ryan walked down the narrow aisles, his eyes scanning titles and authors, searching for books that would acquaint him with Japanese culture, history, and language. He wanted to understand Megumi better - the complex layers of her background that intertwined with the enigma she presented.

His fingers brushed against the spines of the books as he selected a handful on traditional Japanese arts, history of the Samurai, the evolution of Japanese language, and a copy of 'Genji Monogatari.' He also picked up a beginner's guide to learning Japanese. He wished to delve into the nuances of Megumi's heritage, to connect with her on a deeper level than they had ever ventured.

As he made his way to the checkout counter, his heart was filled with a sense of determination. He felt like he had taken the first step on a journey that would bring him closer to Megumi, a journey filled with learning and understanding. This was not just about making a romantic connection; it was about bridging two different worlds, two different cultures. He was ready to commit to this path, ready to learn, ready to immerse himself in Megumi's world.

Back at his apartment, Ryan settled into his favorite reading chair, the stack of books from the bookstore spread out on the coffee table in front of him. He picked up the beginner's guide to the Japanese language first, flipping it open and starting from the very beginning. His eyes scanned the pages, absorbing the strokes of hiragana and katakana, the rhythmic cadence of sentence structures, and the nuances of Japanese honorifics.

When he grew tired, he switched to the history of the Samurai, fascinated by the intriguing blend of martial prowess and philosophical depth that characterized these warriors. He marveled at their dedication, their code of ethics, and the profound influence they had on Japanese society.

Hours passed as Ryan delved into page after page, his mind a whirl of samurai, Shinto shrines, hiragana characters, and tales from 'Genji Monogatari.' The world around him faded as he immersed himself in the heart of Japan, through the written word. The soft glow of the desk lamp illuminated the room as night fell, a testament to Ryan's relentless pursuit of understanding Megumi's roots. His apartment, usually a rather standard bachelor's pad, had tonight transformed into a little sanctuary of Japanese culture and literature.

As the clock struck midnight, Megumi quietly slipped into the serene yoga studio. The hustle and bustle of the day's classes had long since subsided, giving way to a peaceful silence. The instructor, a pretty Japanese woman in her thirties, was meticulously tidying up the room. Upon noticing Megumi, her face lit up with delight, a stark contrast to the muted surroundings.

"Megumi!" she exclaimed, "How long it's been! How have you been?" Her voice reverberated softly through the still, quiet studio, a harmonious blend of warmth and surprise. The last shreds of the day had given way to an unexpected reunion, adding a sweet twist to an otherwise ordinary Saturday night.

The instructor's smile faltered as she noticed the stress lines etching Megumi's usually radiant face. "What's wrong?" she murmured, her voice now carrying a note of concern. "Are you okay?" There was a pause, the silence in the room growing more pronounced. Megumi hesitated, then nodded, "Can we talk?" The calmness in her voice belied the turmoil within, and the yoga studio, usually a haven of peace and tranquility, suddenly became a silent witness to an unfolding story. The instructor, named Maki Tanaka was taken aback. This must be serious.

In all of the years that Megumi has been a member at Maki's club, she had never really opened up. Maki had tried, she has invited her out on multiple occasions, with Megumi politely declining. The only thing that Maki really knew about Megumi is that she was the CEO of a gaming company, and that she lived alone and worked a lot.

In Megumi's highly compartmentalized world, the "friend" box was totally empty. Her years of complete focus and dedication to her work left that one neglected. She respected Maki, and in many ways, she envied her with her fun loving personality and vibrant personal life. She needed a friend's advice, and Maki would have to do.

The two settled into a deep conversation.

CHAPTER TWENTY
Monday

Ryan arrived early at the office, the early morning silence broken only by the distant hum of the city waking up. The anticipation tingled in him like electricity. He settled into his desk, his mind clear and focused. He felt the weight of responsibility on his shoulders. The secret Megumi had shared with him was not just a testament of trust, but a call to action. His role was now not merely that of an employee, but a confidant.

His fingers danced over the keyboard, the code flowing from his mind onto the screen with ease and finesse. He was determined, more than ever, to prove his worth and commitment. The office was still empty, the rest of the team not due for another hour or so. It was a poignant reminder to Ryan of the magnitude of the task at hand.

He had to work hard, to keep his mouth shut, to ensure that Megumi's secret remained within the four walls of his consciousness. He would show Megumi that he was reliable and trustworthy. In the silence of the early morning, Ryan was not just a marketer, but a guardian of trust. The day had just started, and Ryan was more than ready for it.

As the morning gave way to the early afternoon, the office was alive with the hum of activity. The quiet solitude of the early morning was now just a distant memory. Ryan, having barely moved from his desk, finally stood up to stretch his legs. His eyes scanned the office for Megumi but found no sign of her. With a growing sense of unease, he made his way to Jun's desk.

"Hey Jun, have you seen Megumi?" Ryan asked, trying to keep his voice casual. Jun looked up from his work, his face reflecting a similar concern.

"No, I haven't," Jun admitted, pushing his glasses up the bridge of his nose. "It's odd, she's usually the first one here. I tried calling her, but she's not picking up. Nobody's heard from her. We had a meeting scheduled."

Ryan felt a knot of worry form in his stomach. In the bustling office, the absence of Megumi loomed large. The afternoon was getting more complex than Ryan had anticipated. Ryan's emotions danced between concern for his job and concern for the woman he was quickly developing feelings for. A tinge of fear ran through his mind - was she avoiding the office while she planned his firing? Or was she struggling with her own fears and anxiety? He launched a silent prayer for her well being, and a chance for her to find out that her secret was safe with him.

CHAPTER TWENTY-ONE
Friday

Body copy here It was Friday again, a week since that unforgettable encounter at the strip club. Ryan sat in his office, the clutter of papers and coffee cups a stark contrast to the chaos that brewed within him. Megumi's desk, usually buzzing with activity, stood silent and empty. The absence of her daily presence felt like a chasm in the otherwise bustling office.

Ryan found his mind wandering back to the events of the last Friday night. He recalled the shock that had coursed through him when he spotted Megumi under the neon lights, a sight entirely divergent from the Megumi he knew, the stoic and determined CEO.

Each day of her absence this week had intensified Ryan's worry. He wondered if she was dealing with her fears, if she was okay, or if she was planning on never coming back. Was she planning for his removal? He had no idea. He missed her more than he had anticipated, not just as a colleague but as a person he had developed feelings for. The office wasn't the same without her, and neither was he. As he looked at her empty chair, he made a silent promise to himself - to protect her secret and to be there for her, no matter what the future held.

Ryan began to pack his things, his eyes never straying too far from Megumi's vacant desk. As he shuffled his documents into his briefcase, he caught fragments of hushed conversations from the passing colleagues. Whispers of curiosity and theories about Megumi's absence swirled around him like a haze. He heard their conjectures, each hypothesis stranger than the last - from wild clandestine affairs to covert business deals. He pushed all of these thoughts out of his mind as quickly as possible.

But Ryan was not interested in their theories. He had a more personal, more profound connection to Megumi's absence. The whispers only amplified the hollow echo in his heart - the void left by her unexplained absence. He ignored the office chatter, focused on packing up his things. He took one final glance at her desk, the stack of untouched documents awaiting her attention, the silence that hung around it like a specter.

With a heavy heart, he slung his bag over his shoulder, switched off the lights, and walked out of the office. The chatter faded behind him, but his thoughts were filled with concern for Megumi. As the office door closed behind him, the reality of her absence felt more tangible than ever.

Ryan found himself seated at a small ramen restaurant later that evening, the hum of conversation and clinking dishes around him fading into the background. He sat alone at the corner booth, absentmindedly stirring his miso ramen, his thoughts engrossed in Megumi. The rich, steamy broth did nothing to warm the chill that had settled in him since her sudden absence.

Just as he was about to take the first sip, his phone buzzed. It was Megumi. She had sent him a text, breaking her eerie silence. "Meet me outside the club," it read. Ryan's heart fluttered in his chest at her words. He quickly paid for his untouched ramen and rushed out of the restaurant, his heart pounding in rhythm with the neon city lights guiding him towards the ShadowVerse club. Megumi's abrupt message offered a glimmer of hope and mystery that pulled him forward, into the heart of the city's nightlife. As he neared the club, the pulsating music growing louder, he felt a whirlwind of emotions - anticipation, worry, relief, but most of all, the strong desire to see Megumi again.

As Ryan approached the club, Megumi stepped out of the shadows. A serious look on her face. Ryan, butterflies in his stomach, picked up the pace. They are now standing face to face. A long moment passes, neither saying a word. Megumi studying Ryan's eyes. Ryan breaks the silence, "It's good to see you. Is everything okay?" Ryan's pulse quickens as his words hang in the air. She nods, still intently focused on Ryan's eyes. Ryan looks up at the marquis, and back to her, "You wanted to see me?" Again, she nods. She takes a deep breath, "I want to apologize for the other night." Ryan starts to speak but she cuts him off, "I lied to you the other night. I didn't know what to say. I did feel something, something electric when I touched you, and when you looked into my eyes." Ryan is dumbfounded. He has no words. She continues, "This is who I am Ryan. If you can accept that, meet me here at 1 am."

Without another word, she turns and walks over to the side door of the club. A tall and muscular Japanese bouncer bows slightly to her and opens the door. She slips inside of the club while Ryan stands there trying to process what just happened.

CHAPTER TWENTY-TWO

1 AM

As the clock strikes one am, the side door of the ShadowVerse club glides open, spilling a sliver of light onto the dark alleyway. Megumi emerged, her heart pounding in sync with the thumping bass that bled through the club walls. She immediately scans the area and finds Ryan, standing at the curb, his gaze locked onto hers. Somehow things feel different. There is a growing feeling of trust and comfort between the two.

Megumi flashes a slight, yet vulnerable smile, "You came." His eyes are locked with hers as he nods, "Of course. Are you hungry?" She shakes her head slightly, "Not really. If you are though, we can get something." He shakes his head, "I really, I just came to see you." She smiles. "Want to get a drink? So we can talk?" He nods yes.

Ryan and Megumi make their way off of the still buzzing streets and into a small, secluded bar. As they enter, it's clear that Megumi is very comfortable here. Megumi nods to the hostess, a lady in her fifties before making her way over to a secluded booth off in the shadows. As Ryan and Megumi slide into the elegant and secluded booth, the hostess glides over, removes the "reserved" sign from the table and looks to Megumi. Megumi just nods. The hostess looks to Ryan, "What can I get you?" Ryan looks to Megumi, "What are you having?" Megumi speaks softly,

"Vodka Tonic." Ryan looks politely to the hostess, "Two Vodka Tonics, please." The hostess bows slightly and leaves.

The casual and easy feel from outside dissipates, and is replaced with a silent and awkward tension. Ryan looks around, slightly uncomfortable, "How is your night going?" Megumi just nods, "Good, thank you. Yours?" Ryan nods.

The drinks arrive. Megumi holds her glass up to Ryan, "Kampai." They both take a drink.

Megumi takes a deep breath, "Please let me explain why I dance. You're curious about that, right?" Ryan shrugs his shoulders. He is curious, but he doesn't want to force her into an awkward conversation. She continues, "Both of my parents died when I was very young. I was sent here, to Tokyo for school. As I got older, I needed to make money to pay for my education, and dancing was a perfect way." Ryan interjects, "That makes perfect sense." She continues, ".. and now, I just like the club. I like the atmosphere." Ryan nods before asking, "Have you ever.. been married?" She shakes her head, "No, never. Have you?"

Ryan takes a deep breath, "Actually yes, I am in the process of getting divorced now." Megumi's eyes narrow, "So you're married?" He nods yes, "Yes, but it's over. It's very complicated." Ryan feels Megumi slipping away from him, "We were really young. We met in high school. At first things were good, but then over time.. we both just sort of changed." Megumi nods that she understands but in his heart, he feels their earlier connection fading away. Megumi asks, "Do you still love her?" Ryan shakes his head, "I thought that I did, but no. Not anymore. I don't feel anything at all for her. Everything changed." Megumi nods. She flashes Ryan a pained and awkward smile before standing, she looks to him, her voice cold and measured again, "Things don't change that quickly Ryan. I hope you can understand, but I cannot see you anymore. Please don't tell anyone about this night." She turns to leave. Ryan is dumbfounded. He is frozen for a moment before hopping up from the table to pursue her.

Just outside of the bar, Ryan catches up to Megumi. She turns to face him. Ryan is puzzled, "So that's it? You're just shutting me out?" She nods, "What could have changed? Why should I trust that you're even available?" He peers deeply into her eyes, "The moment I saw you. I knew that I loved you. That was the moment that I knew I was done just going through the paces. I knew I wanted more. Something real. I am sick of hurting. I am sick of giving everything to somebody who doesn't care. I am standing here, asking you, to please take a chance on me."

A mix of hurt and fear washed over Megumi's expression. "I wish I could. But I just can't. I hope you can understand." He shakes his head, "I can't."

She is not used to people pushing back on her. He continues, "I am going through with my divorce. That's over. I am going to stay single until you can see that I am here. I am here, and I am all yours. Whether it takes ten days or ten years, I will be here waiting for you."

She stands there, just looking at him. He continues, "I could have lied to you. Told you I was single. My wife is back in L.A. and she is never coming to Japan. But I was honest with you. I will always be honest with you."

She nods before walking away. Ryan stands out on the sidewalk. Despite the fact that Tokyo is one of the most densely populated cities in the world, Ryan has never felt more alone in his entire life.

CHAPTER TWENTY-THREE

Open Season

More than a month had passed since that fateful night when Ryan and Megumi parted ways. Tokyo, with its buzzing life and endless echoes of modernity, resumed its pace, as did their lives. However, the undercurrents of their tumultuous conversation still lingered, creating ripples in their day to day interactions.

Work, as a saving grace, distracted Ryan. His professional commitments pushed him to deliver, keeping his mind off the personal turmoil. He immersed himself in his projects, his focus solely on the tasks at hand.

Megumi, on the other hand, was doing her best to avoid any unnecessary interactions with Ryan. Their professional paths still crossed, but now there was an undeniable distance between them. She made it a point to not attend any meetings where Ryan was present. Her interactions with him were always professional, yet she kept an emotional fortress around her, making her seem distant, aloof even.

Despite the bustling city around him, the crowded offices, and the ceaseless ticking of time, Ryan often found himself alone. His heart longed for an understanding that seemed increasingly elusive. His only consolation was that he was being true to himself, to Megumi, and to the faint glimmer of hope that still resided deep within him. Despite the deep chasm that now separated them, he was determined to wait, even if it took an eternity.

Friday night descended upon the city, painting its high rises with hues of neon lights and vibrant energy. The office was abuzz with the aroma of excitement and anticipation for the night out at the local nightclub, a tradition that had been a part of the corporate culture for as long as anyone could remember. A night of melody and mirth, a night to let go and be a part of the conviviality that Tokyo's nightlife had to offer.

Amidst the pulsing music and flowing drinks, Mika stood out. Her laughter echoed above the din and her animated expressions drew attention. As the night progressed, she seemed to grow bolder, her glances towards Ryan becoming more frequent and laden with an unmistakable intent.

Ryan, however, was intent on maintaining his composure. Despite the waves of attention emanating from Mika, he chose to remain nonchalant, acknowledging her with a polite smile when necessary but refraining from engaging in any intimate discussions. He was aware of his surroundings, yet detached, seemingly lost in the cacophony of karaoke tunes and his own swirling thoughts.

As the night stretched on, Akemi, a close friend of Mika's, sidled up to her, her eyes flicking towards Ryan with a questioning glance. "Would you be upset if I asked Ryan out?" she asked hesitantly. Mika forced a smile, her heart clenching at the question. "Of course not, Akemi," she replied, her voice steady despite the turmoil inside her. "He's his own person, isn't he?" Akemi smiles tentatively, "But you like him too, right?" Mika shakes her head, "He's nice, but no. There is really nothing there. He's all yours." Akemi smiles. The path is cleared for her to proceed.

With this tacit approval, Akemi approached Ryan, her eyes brimming with flirtation and a hint of nervousness. She really wants to land this elusive foreigner. She engaged him in conversation, her words flowing as smoothly as the drinks that night. Ryan, true to his character, responded with polite nods and courteous smiles. He was attentive and respectful, but there was a certain distance in his eyes, a wall Akemi could simply not scale. His heart was clearly elsewhere, lost in the labyrinth of his own thoughts and feelings. All he could do was think of Megumi and the silent promise he made - both to himself and Megumi. Their connection was unmistakable. She just needed her to recognize it.

As the night wound down, Akemi returned to Mika, her hopeful eyes now clouded with confusion. "Mika," she began, her voice tinged with disappointment, "Ryan is not going to happen." Mika looked surprised but quickly masked it with a comforting smile, "Why do you say that?" she asked. Akemi sighed, "He's a million miles away." Mika shrugged, trying to look nonchalant, "Maybe he's just not ready for a relationship." Inside, however, her heart was racing. The revelation was unexpected, yet it added another layer of complexity to the already tangled web of emotions. While she felt a pang of sympathy for her friend, she couldn't help but feel a spark of hope for her own unvoiced feelings for Ryan.

Ryan excused himself, getting up from the bustling table and sauntering down the long hall to the restroom. He needed a moment - a break from the confusing world of social interactions and unspoken emotions. As he left the table, Mika's eyes followed him. A surge of resolution coursed through her veins. She rose from her chair and trailed him at a safe distance, waiting for him in the dimly lit hallway.

When Ryan emerged, he was taken aback to find Mika leaning against the wall, her eyes determined, her posture radiating an unexpected intensity. He blinked, his heart beating faster, "Mika?" he questioned. She took a deep breath, her gaze meeting his. "Ryan," her voice was soft yet steady, "I need to tell you something..." This was it. Mika was going to make her plea, her final attempt to breach the walls surrounding Ryan's heart. She comes off of the wall, and steps up close to him. Her eyes peer into his, "I want you Ryan. Do you want me. There is no need for both of us to be alone tonight." He looks at Mika and takes a deep breath, "You're very pretty Mika. And smart. You are what any guy would want. But I am just not in that place." She processes this, "Are you.. not into girls?" He chuckles, "No, I am into girls." She gets frustrated. The drinks from the night have added up, "Then what is it? Is it me? Is it something about me that disgusts you?" He takes another deep breath, "It's complicated." She is not letting him off the hook, "Can you explain it for me?"

Mika returns to the table and Akemi looks puzzled, "What's up? Were you talking with Ryan?" Mika nods. Akemi persists, "And?" Mika shakes her head. "He's already in love. Not available." Akemi is puzzled, "He told you that? With who?" Again, Mika shakes her head, "No idea. All he said that is that he is in love with somebody that doesn't feel the same for him." Akemi has been drinking for hours and she is not very subtle as she processes this. She is formulating a plan in her head. Mika notices, "Seriously. He's not available." Akemi nods as she thinks this through.

Ryan is sitting in a booth with a few of his male co-workers. He is watching a couple of his colleagues, up on stage, butchering the English language as they perform "Just like Heaven" by the Cure. He suddenly checks his watch, hurriedly drops some Yen on the table and asks his friends to pay up his tab. He hops up and leaves the lounge quickly.

CHAPTER TWENTY-FOUR
Private Eye(s)

Ryan steps into the cool night, the bright lights of the city dancing off the rain-soaked streets. He pulls his coat tighter around him, the chill seeping into his bones as he crosses the road to a narrow alley-way. Glancing once more at his watch, he positions himself in the shadows, out of sight, across from the side door of the Shadow Verse club. His heart hammers in his chest as his eyes dart across the club's entrance, taking in every detail, every face that emerges.

The night is filled with a cacophony of city sounds— blaring horns, distant laughter, the hum of late-night commerce. But within Ryan, there is a silence, a singular focus. His eyes, keen and unyielding, do not miss a beat. He looks like a private detective out of a noir film, a lone wolf on a personal mission. The city's secrets lay bare before him, their shadows dancing across his face. Each minute he spends in the shadows deepens the mystery he is entangled in, pulling him deeper into a world that makes less and less sense.

Thirty minutes have passed. In the dimly lit alleyway across from the club, Ryan finds solace in the shadows, a place now familiar to him. His gaze fixates on the side door of Shadow Verse, the spot where Megumi, like a nocturnal blossom, emerges at the end of her shift. The scene has unfolded under his watchful eyes every Friday night since their last, deliciously painful encounter. There's a blend of nostalgia and a guardian's resolve in his presence. Silently, he watches, an unseen sentinel, ensuring that Megumi's journey from the doorway to her car is safe and untroubled, a ritual of care and protection in the quiet night.

Just as the clock hits 1 AM, like a specter materializing from the depths, Megumi steps out of the club. The harsh neon club lights soften as they spill onto her, painting a picture Ryan would not forget. He watches, unseen, as she glides into a waiting town car. The city lights reflect off the glossy black paint as the car pulls away, leaving a trail of exhaust and mystery in its wake.

Ryan hesitates for a moment, still cloaked in the alleyway's shadows, the image of Megumi etched in his mind. He then steps out, the crunch of gravel under his boots echoing in the deserted alley. He takes one last look at the retreating vehicle, then turns and begins his walk home, the city's secrets wrapping around him like the winter chill.

As Ryan enters his high-end apartment, the silence is overwhelming. The hollowness of his luxurious abode seems to echo his solitude. His footsteps, muffled by the plush carpet, are the only sound in the expansive, open-plan living room that is adorned with minimalist furniture. High above the bustling city, his apartment offers a panoramic view of Tokyo's sprawling skyline.

He makes his way to the large glass window, hands in his pockets, eyes pensive. He stares out into the sea of neon lights, the city's veins illuminated in the darkness, pulsating rhythmically. The hushed whispers of the city at night float up to his apartment, a stark contrast to the mirth and noise from the club earlier. He places a hand on the cool glass, his reflection superimposed on the cityscape. His lonely figure, surrounded by the vibrant life of Tokyo, paints a strikingly poignant picture. His mind, still filled with the night's events, holds onto the ghost of Megumi's image, a phantom in the city of neon lights.

Megumi slips into her penthouse, the soft click of the door barely a whisper in the vast space. She sets down her belongings on the sleek, polished countertop of her open kitchen. The room is bathed in the soft, warm light of carefully placed fixtures, casting a golden glow. Her heels tap a quiet rhythm on the marble floor as she crosses towards the large floor-to-ceiling window, her elegant silhouette framed against the backdrop of Tokyo.

She places her hands on the window ledge, her gaze drawn to the dance of colors and lights below. The city, a pulsating kaleidoscope of neon, stretches out in all directions. The skyscrapers tower like sentinels, their lit windows mirroring the stars twinkling overhead. Her heart echoes with the rhythm of the city, a symphony of life and energy that intertwines with her own. Her figure is a solitary shadow against the vibrant cityscape, a mirror image of the man she left behind, both captivated by the same panorama of mesmerizing lights. In the quiet solitude, Megumi's thoughts intertwine with the distant hum of Tokyo and quiet thoughts of Ryan.

In another part of Tokyo, Ryan is still standing at his window, thinking of Megumi.

CHAPTER TWENTY-FIVE
Overheard

Megumi finds herself standing by the cubicles, engaged in a casual conversation with one of the personnel from accounting. As the lady recounts a humorous incident involving an expense report, Megumi's laughter punctuates the monotonous hum of office chatter. Then, abruptly, her attention is caught by an overlapping conversation between Mika and Akemi, two colleagues from the marketing department.

She hears Ryan's name, and the tone of their conversation piqued her interest. She strains her ears, her attention shifting from the accounting anecdote to the girl's discussion. She hears them talk about how they approached Ryan, hoping to kick off a romantic relationship. But according to their conversation, Ryan had turned them down gently but firmly, indicating that his heart was spoken for.

Megumi's heartbeat quickens as she covertly listens, her exchange with the accounting lady fading into a dull drone. She absorbs Mika and Akemi's words, her mind racing to decipher the implications. As they continue their conversation, oblivious to her eavesdropping, it becomes clear to Megumi: Ryan, isolated in his high-rise overlooking Tokyo, is in love with her. And though the girls don't mention any names, she can't help but hope that she is the subject of his secret affections.

Megumi wraps up her conversation with the lady from accounting, her heart pounding in her chest. The lady's story has ended, but she barely notices, her mind still on the overheard conversation from moments ago. With a polite nod, she steps away from the cubicles and returns to the sanctity of her own office.

As she walks, she passes by the glass doors of Ryan's office. She hesitates for a moment before she musters the courage to glance inside. He is there, alone, absorbed in some paperwork. Feeling bold, she smiles at him through the glass. Their eyes meet, and for a split second, time seems to stand still.

Ryan looks up at that exact moment, his gaze meeting Megumi's. A brief spark of surprise flickers across his face, replaced quickly by a warm smile. There's a mutual understanding, an unspoken sentiment fluttering in the space between them. It's a moment that lasts barely a second but feels like an eternity. As Megumi walks away, she can't help but replay the moment in her mind, feeling a tingling sensation that she associates with the beginning of something beautiful.

Outside, soft droplets of rain begin to fall, tapping lightly against the windows of the office building. The sky is a panoramic canvas of dark, ominous clouds, their threatening presence casting long shadows over Tokyo. Thunder growls in the distance, a primal roar that echoes through the monolithic structures of steel and glass. The cityscape flickers under the sporadic bursts of lightning, revealing a world momentarily paused under the impending storm. Peering out of the window, Megumi watches as the streets transform into a glossy tableau, reflections dancing on the rain-soaked pavement. It is clear: the night ahead promises to be a wet and stormy one, a perfect backdrop to the emotional turbulence brewing within the confines of the office.

Ryan steps outside, standing under the vast overhang of the colossal office building, just on the edge of the rain's reach. He holds an umbrella by his side, its purpose defeated under the protective shelter of the architecture. The rain intensifies, a melodic symphony accompanying the night's drama. He watches as Megumi bursts from the building's entrance, oblivious to the rain she is now immersed in, as if her confrontation with nature is a necessary purification ritual.

She walks hurriedly towards the curb, her coat providing little protection against the relentless downpour. Her head is tilted upwards, her eyes scanning the streets for the hopeful glow of an approaching taxi. Her hair clings to her face, dark strands pasted onto her skin by the rain. She is soaked, yet there's a certain resilience in her posture, a determination that renders the rain a mere triviality. Meanwhile, Ryan, safely ensconced from the rain, observes this scene unfold, the unused umbrella in his hand feeling heavier by the second.

A succession of taxi cabs pass by, their lights casting fleeting shadows on Megumi's determined face. Each one either occupied or too hurried to stop in the relentless downpour. As she steps back, momentarily defeated, Ryan makes his move. He rushes towards her, the deluge soaking his clothes and extinguishing the protective shield of his corporate facade. He extends the umbrella over her, the gesture puncturing the tension that had been stretched between them.

Megumi looks at him, surprise etched on her face, drowned by the rain yet illuminated by the flickering lights of the city. Her eyes, raw and unguarded, meet his. The umbrella, although drenched and slightly askew, serves as a symbolic barrier against the storm, both literally and figuratively. Their shared silence speaks volumes, the chaos of the storm serving as a fitting soundtrack to the unfolding drama.

Raising his free hand, Ryan hails a cab that's approaching. The bright yellow vehicle pulls to a stop beside them, its tires spraying water onto the drenched sidewalk. Ryan opens the door, holding the umbrella steady above Megumi's head. Her gaze locks onto him, surprise mingling with subtle relief. He has become her unexpected shelter amidst the storm, an oasis in the urban deluge.

Swallowing her surprise, Megumi looks to Ryan, "I will catch the next one." Ryan shakes his head, "I need to go back in. I was just taking a break." She looks at him, her eyes staring into his. He continues, "I just didn't want to see you getting soaked. Here.." he hands her the umbrella. The taxi cab driver looks at the two impatiently. Megumi accepts the umbrella and slips into the cab. Before closing the door, she looks at Ryan. She so desperately wants to ask him about the conversation she overheard between Mika and Akemi. The words simply won't come out. She wants to invite Ryan into the cab. Still she is paralyzed. Her fear, her uncertainties are visible on her face. This is so out of character for her. Ryan looks around and then back to her, "Please get home safe. Have a good night." She nods, "Thank you. You too." As he starts to close the door she adds tenderly, "Please don't work too late." He nods politely.

As the taxi pulls away from the curb and slowly migrates into the flow of traffic, Megumi looks back at Ryan. Their eyes meet. They hold their gaze for what feels like an eternity. An unspoken connection re-ignited. They both know that life will never again be the same. Ryan, oblivious to the rain that is now soaking his hair, face and clothes watches as the cab disappears from sight.

Ryan turns, his gaze falling on the imposing structure that is his workplace. He barely registers the chilling rain seeping into his clothes as he trudged back inside. The office is eerily quiet, the only sound being the distant hum of the air conditioning paired with the quiescent tapping of his shoes against the polished floor. He makes his way to his office, each step echoing his thoughts of Megumi.

He enters his office, the motion sensor lights flickering on, bathing the room in a soft glow that battles the shadows of the storm-tossed night. His clothes are damp, sticking to his skin; a result of his well-timed break and fateful encounter. With a sigh, he walks over to the large window adorning his office wall. The cityscape is streaked with rain, a vague reflection of his current state of mind. He finds himself wondering about Megumi, her words replaying in his mind.

He rests his hand on the cool glass, his eyes fixed on the city illuminated by sporadic flashes of lightning. Thoughts of Megumi flood his mind, a torrent as wild and unpredictable as the storm outside. His heart beats a rhythm of uncertainty, a silent echo of the questions he has about their re-ignited connection. As the storm rages on, the echo of her words fills the room, "Please don't work too late." And in that moment, he feels a resolve strengthened within him. This storm, like his feelings, won't last forever. For now, though, he allows himself to get lost in the tempest, in thoughts of her.

The door to Megumi's penthouse swings open with a gentle push, the soft carpet swallowing the sound of her entrance. She steps inside, her slender fingers unclasping the umbrella she carries. The umbrella, a tangible reminder of Ryan's sweet and selfless gesture, receives a gentle stroke from Megumi's hand as she places it on a stand by the door. A small smile tugs at the corners of her mouth as she hangs her coat next to the umbrella, her mind filled with thoughts of Ryan.

She walks over to the towering windows, an unobstructed view of Tokyo's skyline stretching out before her. The storm outside mirrors the tempest of emotions within her, each lightning streak echoing the electricity she felt in Ryan's presence. She watches as raindrops trace paths down the glass, their journey as erratic and unpredictable as the connection she shares with Ryan.

Lost in thought, she lets out a soft sigh, her breath fogging up the window momentarily before disappearing as quickly as it came. The storm continues to rage outside, its fury and passion only rivaled by the emotions coursing through her. In the solitude of her penthouse and in the eye of the storm, Megumi finds herself dwelling on the rekindled relationship, much like Ryan did in his office. The echo of their shared past, along with the promise of a shared future, fills the luxurious penthouse as the night grows darker. The final scene of the chapter fades out on her silhouette against the backdrop of Tokyo's storm-lit skyline, a poignant end to their day.

Chapter Twenty-Six

The Umbrella

Ryan dashed into the office, much later than usual. His heart pounded in his chest, the echo of his late-night conversation with Megumi reverberating in his mind. He tried to smooth down his tie, his fingers trembling slightly from the whirlwind of emotions. Anxious to hide his inner turmoil, he forced a smile onto his face, nodding a quick hello to his colleagues as he passed them. His usually punctual arrival had shifted to a frantic rush this morning, a deviation that didn't go unnoticed by his perceptive coworkers. Swiftly, he entered his office, the familiar surroundings providing a semblance of calm in the brewing storm of his thoughts.

As he settled behind his desk, something unfamiliar caught his eye. Propped up against his desk drawers stood an umbrella, its sleek design immediately setting it apart from the rest of his office decor. It wasn't the umbrella he gave to Megumi, but a new one. Intriguingly beautiful, evidently expensive, it called out to him. Compelled by its allure, he picked it up, his fingers making contact with its silky fabric. The texture was sublime, a testament to its high-quality craftsmanship. As he ran his fingers along its surface, a faint scent tickled his senses, a scent that was strangely familiar. He brought his fingers closer to his nose, the subtle perfume wafting from them. It was a scent he had come to associate with Megumi, a hint of her presence in his personal space. A smile came across his face.

As he smiled, Megumi appeared in his doorway. Immaculately dressed and coiffed to perfection. A far cry from the wet version of her he tucked into the cab just last night. He looks up and she smiles sweetly, "I'm sorry, I wanted to return the one you gave me last night, but I must have left it in the cab." Ryan doesn't know what to say. Her sudden appearance has him even more shaken than being late. He adds, "Oh, no problem, I wanted you to keep it." She smiles as she slides gracefully into his office and sits in the chair in front of his desk. She raises her eyebrows, "Apologies for the perfume. I spilled some on it before leaving home." This was obviously a little white lie. She put it on there on purpose, so he would think of her. He knew it and she could tell. He just smiles, "It smells great. What scent is that?" She smiles gracefully, "It's Miss Dior, Blooming Bouquet. You like it?" He nods, "I do. It smells amazing."

She stands up and looks at him. A seductive look in her eye. "Thank you for last night. That was really sweet of you." He just smiles. She turns and leaves. His previously chaotic morning has taken a decidedly romantic turn. He props the umbrella back against his desk and takes a smell from his fingers one last time before diving into his work.

The day wore on, Ryan's attention devoted to the avalanche of emails and reports that sought his attention. His eyes were glued to the bright glow of his computer screen, his fingers flying across the keyboard in a rhythmic pattern, an artificial symphony of productivity.

Just when he was engrossed in outlining his presentation for the upcoming meeting, an instant message notification popped up on the corner of his screen. It was from Megumi: "Dinner?". The message was simple, but the implications were anything but. A smile tugged at the corners of his mouth as he quickly replied, "definitely."

CHAPTER TWENTY-SEVEN

Bridges

Under the twinkling lights of Shibuya, a vibrant hub of Tokyo, Megumi and Ryan found themselves seated in an elegant restaurant. The sophisticated ambiance was matched only by the exquisite fusion cuisine that the restaurant was famous for. The soft glow of the hanging lanterns bathed the room in a warm light, illuminating the delicate pieces of sushi meticulously arranged on their plates.

Across the table, they exchanged glances over sake cups. Ryan found himself entranced by her, his heart pounding like the vibrant city that surrounded them. Their conversation flowed as smoothly as the sake in their cups, ranging from light-hearted banter to profound life discussions.

As the evening wore on, the city lights outside the restaurant seemed to dance in harmony with the rhythm of their conversation. The connection between them was palpable, a bridge that transcended cultural and geographical boundaries. Back in his home country, Ryan could never have imagined a moment like this - under the Tokyo sky, sharing sushi and stories with Megumi. Yet, there he was, living what felt like a beautifully crafted dream.

CHAPTER TWENTY-EIGHT
Along the Sumida River

After leaving the restaurant, Ryan and Megumi found themselves meandering along a walkway skirting the massive Sumida River. The night skies of Tokyo were remarkably clear, a vast canvas sprinkled with distant stars. The city lights on either side of the river sparkled, their reflections dancing upon the gentle waves.

Ryan felt the cool breeze that swept across the water, rustling the leaves of the trees lining the walkway. The sounds of the bustling city were muffled here, replaced by the soothing murmur of the river. Walking side by side, their silhouettes were cast on the stone pathway by the soft glow of the sporadically placed street lamps. Their laughter and shared quiet moments echoed along the serene riverbank, adding their unique melody to the symphony of the night. Megumi stops, pulling herself in close to Ryan's chest. This is their first date, but they look like they have been together forever. Their eyes are locked and the physical tension between them is palpable. With a vulnerable look, she peers deep into his eyes, "I have wanted this for so long." He smiles and nods, "Me too." With that, he shifts forward and they begin to kiss.

As their lips met in a passionate embrace, everything else faded into insignificance. The kiss was a fervent exchange of unspoken feelings, a culmination of the tension that had been building between them all evening. The cool breeze, the rustling leaves, and the distant murmur of the city all seemed to hush, as though nature itself was paying homage to their moment. Their hearts pounded in sync, echoing the rhythm of their kiss. Ryan held Megumi close, losing himself in the sweetness and intensity of this moment. A wave of tenderness washed over Megumi, leaving her breathless. The intensity of their kiss was a testament to the connection they shared, a promise of the deep bond that was slowly taking root between them.

As they slowly pulled away from their impassioned kiss, the air was filled with the intoxicating scent of Megumi's perfume. The Miss Dior perfume, a vibrant symphony of floral notes, left an enchanting trail, further enhancing the aura of romance that surrounded them. The top notes of Calabrian bergamot, mixed with the elegant Grasse rose, merged seamlessly with the subtle hints of fresh roses, presenting a harmonious blend of freshness and warmth. The lingering aroma of patchouli in the base notes added an earthy depth to the perfume, exuding an allure that was as captivating as Megumi herself. The fragrance was a reflection of her personality - elegant, spirited, and truly unforgettable.

Drawing her closer, Ryan gently nestled his nose against the curve of her neck, inhaling deeply. The scent of her perfume, intertwining with her natural essence, was intoxicating. A soft whisper escaped his lips, "You smell amazing, Megumi... like a beautiful spring morning." His breath warmed her skin, causing a shiver of delight to run through her. He pulled back to look into her eyes, his own reflecting an intense emotion. "I'll never forget this moment," he confessed, his voice barely above a whisper, the sincerity in his words resonating deeply within her. The night, their closeness, the scent of her perfume, and the echo of his words, all imprinted an indelible memory in his heart.

Breaking their intimate moment, Megumi gently touched Ryan's arm and whispered, "We should start walking back to the train station." The words hung in the air, a subtle reminder of the world outside their enchanted bubble. Ryan nodded, understanding the necessity, "Yeah, it's getting late. Let me get us a car though. I'll drop you off." She smiles sweetly and nods. Ryan gets his phone out and opens up an app to call a car, "Let's head over this way. The car can pick us up over here."

As Ryan and Megumi began to navigate their way towards the bustling street corner, the city lights illuminating their path, an unusual aura seemed to loom in the air around them. Their light-hearted chatter dimmed as the shadows of two men stretched out to them from an adjacent alleyway. Stepping into the pool of light from a nearby lamppost, the men were revealed in their full menacing stance. Dressed in crisp suits, their appearances were deceptively sophisticated, but the cold glint in their eyes narrated a story far from sophistication. The intricate tattoos peeking out from under their sleeves were a distinct signature of their affiliation with the Yakuza. They were young, probably in their mid-20's, yet their hardened expressions spoke of experiences far beyond their years. Ryan subtly moved to position himself protectively before Megumi, a sense of unease creeping into the air. They looked past Ryan, locking eyes with Megumi. One of the young Yakuza spoke in a tone that was somehow polite and ominous at the same time, "It's nice to see you." Megumi nodded, trying to hide her fear, "Nice to see you too."

Ryan stood his ground, his mind racing as he tried to decipher the cryptic exchange between Megumi and the two Yakuza. He could feel a tension, a familiarity that seemed oddly out of place. His eyes darted between Megumi and the two men, searching for clues in their interaction. Megumi's polite but guarded response, the thinly veiled threat in the Yakuza's words, and the unspoken understanding that seemed to pass between them - everything pointed towards a backstory that Ryan was unaware of. The seconds dragged into what felt like an eternity as the three of them stood locked in this unusual standoff, the city's cacophony fading into a distant hum. Eventually, it was the Yakuza who broke the silence with an unnerving chuckle, "Nice to meet you." He extends his hand to Ryan cautiously shakes it. With that, the two Yakuza walk off into the night. Ryan looks at Megumi, the romance of the night now replaced with unanswered questions.

As the tension from their unexpected encounter lingering, an elegant black town car pulled up to the curb. Ryan, still processing the interaction, found himself surprised yet again as Megumi took the lead, guiding him into the luxurious vehicle. The cityscape rushed by in a kaleidoscope of lights as they drove, the car's plush interior insulating them from the hustle and bustle outside.

After what felt like an eternity, the car pulled up to a towering, contemporarily designed building that screamed opulence. Megumi stepped out and turned to Ryan. With an air of vulnerability, "Would you like to come up?" Ryan is surprised and he hesitates. Before he can speak, she adds, "I really don't want to be alone." He nods. These were the first words either had spoken during the entirety of the long ride to her place.

CHAPTER TWENTY-NINE

Beginnings

Ryan and Megumi stepped into the luxury penthouse, an expanse of artful sophistication and understated opulence. As the door slowly closed behind them, the sounds of the city were replaced by a hush of serene tranquility. They slipped off their shoes, as is customary in Japanese culture, their footsteps softly echoing on the pristine marble floor. The penthouse was tastefully furnished, with minimalist décor accentuating the high ceilings and expansive glass windows that offered an unending panorama of the city. The soft glow of carefully placed mood lighting bathed the space in warmth, casting long, dancing shadows that played along the walls.

Megumi moved gracefully through the space, a silhouette enhanced by the dim light. Ryan followed, each step revealing another facet of Megumi's world; a world that was as intriguing as it was intimidating. But beneath the surface, there was also a sense of homeliness, a hidden layer of comfort that seemed to extend an unspoken welcome to Ryan. Their journey began in silence, punctuated only by the occasional whisper of fabric against skin, the ticking of a distant clock, and the heavy rhythm of their own hearts.

As they continued their silent exploration, Megumi glanced towards Ryan, her eyes lingering on his still-clad jacket. A gentle smile played on her lips as she broke the silence, "Your jacket, Ryan... I can hang it up for you if you'd like." Ryan, momentarily caught off guard, nodded, slipping off his jacket with a swift, fluid motion. The jacket, a mere piece of fabric, suddenly felt like a symbol of trust passed from one hand to another. With the jacket in her possession, Megumi gracefully crossed the room, her silhouette once again dancing with the dim light. She hung it carefully, each movement seeming like a choreographed dance. The room returned to its silent tranquility, the city's whispers fading once again into the background.

Ryan still had so many questions. Who were the Yakuza and how do they know Megumi. He feels he knows but he fears to hear the answer. As he ponders, Megumi reads him.

"Those men. On the street." she says, and watches for Ryan's response. He nods. She continues, "I need to be honest with you. About who I am." The mood in the room suddenly heavy. Ryan nervously tries to intercept her, "If it's private.." She shakes her head. Cautiously, she proceeds, "I want you to know everything about me, my background, my life.. everything. If you are still interested in me then I know it's real." Ryan nods solemnly. She motions to the couch, "Let's sit?"

They sit down on the elegant, overstuffed leather couch. She is visibly nervous. Ryan waits. After what felt like an eternity, she launches into it, "I lied to you, when I said my parents were both dead. That wasn't true. My parents are both very much alive. Living outside of Kyoto." Ryan listens intently as she continues, "My father, he was a Yakuza. Shinohara-kai. Just like his father. My mom was very young when he met her. She was just nineteen. He took over a nightclub where she was a hostess and they fell in love."

Ryan listens intently. She continues. Emotion choking her voice, "They had me, and then a year later, they had my brother. Everything was good for a while, but my father was already married so he did not live with us. It was very difficult on my mom. She told him that he needed to leave his wife so we could all be together. And he did. It was a huge disgrace and he was forced to leave the Yakuza."

Ryan is puzzled, "Because he got a divorce? I thought.." She shakes her head, "Not divorce. That was not the problem. He was married to the daughter of a boss in another family. His own Oyabun, or father figure in the organization, made him leave when he did this. He can't come back to Tokyo. He disgraced his boss and his family."

Ryan is trying to piece this all together, "And those guys.. tonight?" Megumi shakes her head, "They would never hurt me. Not physically. They just wanted me to know that they saw me. Sometimes that hurts more than physical pain."

Ryan nods as he processes this.'

She continues, "As you would say in America, I am damaged goods." Ryan shakes his head, he stares into her eyes, "No, you are not. Not at all." She nods, "Yes Ryan, yes, I am. You don't understand. Family name in Japan is everything. Mine is filled with shame and disloyalty."

Ryan argues, "Disloyalty? Disloyalty to a crime family? Your dad was loyal to you. Loyal to your mom.. and your brother." She nods, but not really agreeing with him. She looks at Ryan with a mix of vulnerability and hope. As if her entire life hangs in the balance of her next words, "I have never.. been in a relationship. I could not bring myself to tell anybody this story. That's why I dance."

Ryan is confused, "Why you dance?" She nods. "I have never... been intimate with a man. Dancing has been the closest thing to..." her words hang in the air. The sentence is unfinished. Ryan interjects, "Intimacy?" She nods. They both chuckle. Ryan playfully asks, "Or a woman?" She shakes her head, a playfully disgusted look, "No Ryan, never." They chuckle.

After a long pause, she continues, "Are you disgusted by me?" He shakes his head, "Disgusted by you? No, definitely not disgusted by you." He chuckles. She takes his hand and looks deeply into his eyes, "I needed to tell you my story. The whole story. Just so you know who I really am." He nods. She continues, "I gave my notice at the club. I am not a dancer there anymore."

She watches his expression closely for a reaction. His mind races, "You did?" She nods, "The night you gave me your umbrella. I knew you were the one for me." His heart was pounding in his chest. He thought it may have been beating so hard, it may have actually been visible through his Ralph Lauren dress shirt. If this was a dream, he prayed to never wake up. He took a deep breath. She smiles, a look of pure vulnerability and tenderness, "I love you Ryan. Do you love me?" He nods yes, "I do love you. More than life itself."

They lean in and start kissing passionately. Ryan rolls over on top of her on the couch. They kiss for a solid minute before Ryan sits up, "Wow." She smiles a smile like never before. She takes a deep breath, "How about a drink?" He nods yes, "A drink would be great." She sits up and looks over to the elegant bar on the other side of the kitchen. He notices, and stands, "Let me get it."

He makes his way from the couch over to the bar area. Leaning against the bar, previously out of sight is his umbrella. He grins as he picks it up and holds for her to see, "The umbrella I gave you was gone, huh?" He laughs. She calls out from the other room, "That was the last lie."

He returns to the couch with a couple of glasses of whiskey on the rocks. He hands one to her. She chuckles, "Your umbrella.. no way was I giving it back. It was the best gift anybody ever gave me.. and it smelled like you."

He grins, "And the umbrella you gave me, I smelled your perfume all over it." She shakes her head, "Okay I promise now, that was the last lie. I put my perfume on it so you wouldn't forget who gave it to you." They each take a sip of the high end Japanese whiskey from their elegant glasses. He grins, "And that was the best gift that anyone has ever given me. Because it came from you.. and because it smelled like you. And there was no way I would have ever forgotten about you. Even if you never spoke to me again."

As they sat on the couch the world had never felt so beautiful and romantic.

They share a tender smile. Megumi breaking the silence, "Spend the night with me?" He nods yes.

CHAPTER THIRTY

Let's Stay in Bed?

As the morning sun breaks through the window, Ryan and Megumi find themselves entwined in each other's arms. They wake up slowly, their movements languid and unhurried. Ryan opens his eyes first and gazes at her sleeping face, her features softened by the early morning light. His heart swells with love and adoration. Yesterday wasn't a dream. It was real. As real as the woman in his arms.

Ryan leans in, placing a tender kiss on her forehead. She stirs, a small smile spreading across her face as she opens her eyes and sees him. She reaches out, tracing his features with a gentle finger. They are still very much in love, their feelings as palpable as the warmth between them.

Pulling away reluctantly, Ryan swings his legs over the side of the bed, preparing to return to his place to get ready for work. But before he could stand, he feels her hand on his arm. "Stay," Megumi murmurs, her voice soft and alluring, tugging him back into bed.

Her persuasive eyes twinkle with a mischievous charm. "Take the day off," she adds, her fingers drawing idle circles on his bare arm. "We can stay in bed... just the two of us."

Ryan finds himself considering her proposition, the prospect of spending the entire day in bed with her, too tempting to resist. Despite the pressing obligations of the day, he realizes that the woman beside him is his priority. And with that thought, he slips back under the covers, wrapping her in his arms. Work can wait. Today, they have all the time in the world for each other.

At 4pm, well after the usual hustle and bustle of the morning rush, Ryan finally makes his entrance at the office. The once raucous workspace, now subdued, is filled with the soft clicking of keyboards and murmured phone conversations. He tiptoes through the maze of cubicles, hoping to go unnoticed. However, a few raised eyebrows and pointed glances greet him, making him smile sheepishly. He offers no explanation, no apologies, his blithe demeanor speaking volumes.

Upon reaching his desk, Ryan takes a moment to gaze at the organized chaos that is his workspace. He powers on the computer, its familiar hum a comforting reminder of a routine disrupted, yet not entirely forgotten. Before him, a mountain of paperwork awaits, a gentle reminder of the workday he missed. Yet, his mind races back to the morning, to the warmth of the sun, the comfort of the bed, and the woman he left behind.

He settles in his chair, his mind split between the pressing tasks at hand and the precious memories of the day. Despite the urgent workload, Ryan finds himself smiling, the day's delay not a regret but a cherished moment. He starts sifting through the papers, his fingers dancing over the keys, a newfound energy propelling him to finish his work. After all, he has a compelling reason to rush home. Late as it may be, he still has a lot to accomplish, both personally and professionally.

The office clock ticks on, oblivious to the passage of hours, until only the echo of the day's activities fills the room. The once bustling workspace is now a ghostly tableau of empty chairs and darkened screens. Ryan, however, is still there, his silhouette the only evidence of life amidst the stillness. He continues to work, the rhythmic tapping of his fingers on the keyboard serving as the night's monotone serenade.

Suddenly, his cell phone vibrates, breaking the silence. It's Megumi. He picks up the call, her voice carrying the tender lilt that he's come to love. She asks if he can come back to her place, a hint of yearning in her tone. She also suggests that he packs a bag for another overnight stay. A rush of warmth floods his heart at her words. It seems that the universe agrees with them, offering another chance to bask in each other's company without the constraints of time or duty.

Ryan stares at the screen, the unattended documents losing their urgency. He turns off the computer and begins to pack his bag. The usual rush of the workday is replaced by a sweet anticipation. He takes one last look at the deserted office before stepping into the darkness, embraced by a sense of wholeness and contentment. The promise of another night with Megumi fuels him. After all, he has an entire night to look forward to and a love story to continue.

On his way home, Ryan makes a detour to a quaint little sweet shop that is well known and highly thought of to Tokyo locals. The shop, aglow with soft, warm light, welcomes him into its embrace of sweet aromas. The owner, a wise old man with a kind and knowing smile, greets him. Recognizing Ryan as a frequent customer, he selects an assortment of the shop's best sellers—delicate macarons, rich truffles, and some matcha-flavored mochi. The sweets are carefully arranged and packed into an elegant box, the colors of the morsels creating a vibrant medley of delights.

After bidding the shop owner a grateful farewell, Ryan heads back to his place. The box rests securely in his grip, its contents a symbol of his affection and thoughtfulness. The anticipation of Megumi's delight brings a smile to his face as he begins to pack for another cherished night together.

As he weaves through the bustling Tokyo streets, Ryan's phone vibrates against his pocket, jolting him out of his thoughts. Upon seeing Megumi's name flashing on the screen, his heart skips a beat and a smile instantly spreads across his face. He answers, her sweet voice immediately filling him with warmth. She's eager to see him, and in her excitement she's already planning dinner. But for Ryan, it's not about the food. "Just pick whatever you want, Meg," he tells her. "I don't care about what we eat as long as I'm with you." He could almost see her blush at his words, their connection transcending the physical distance between them. He continues on his way, his steps lighter and his heart fuller, knowing that every step takes him closer to Megumi.

As Ryan reached the entrance of Megumi's lavish penthouse, he could feel his heart fluttering with anticipation. The door swung open to reveal Megumi standing in the doorway, the epitome of casual elegance. Dressed in sleek black yoga pants paired with a soft pink hoodie, she emanated a sense of effortless chic. The stark white running shoes added a sporty touch to her relaxed attire. Her hair, usually cascading down her shoulders, was pulled back into a neat ponytail, highlighting her radiant face. Even in such simple attire, she managed to look stunningly beautiful, a grace that Ryan found enchantingly alluring. His eyes met hers, mirroring the deep affection and mutual admiration they held for each other. With a warm but cautious smile, she asks, "Do I look okay?" He is stunned by how good she looks in casual clothing. He shakes his head, "You look better than okay. You look amazing." She smiles, barely able to contain her joy, "I missed you." She hugs him tightly.

An hour had passed, and now they found themselves in a small local restaurant, the aroma of ramen filling the cozy space. Ryan and Megumi, seated across from each other, were engrossed in their own world. The bowl of ramen in front of them, steaming hot and aromatic, was left momentarily forgotten as they lost themselves in each other's eyes. Their relationship, although new, had a comfortable familiarity to it, as if their souls had known each other for a lifetime. Their laughter echoed in the quaint restaurant, their conversations flowing effortlessly. The patrons couldn't help but steal glances at them, their faces glowing with intertwined joy and affection. The couple looked so good together, their happiness was almost infectious. Megumi's eyes, radiant as morning sun, met Ryan's. There was a silent promise in them, a promise of a future filled with shared laughter, shared dreams, and shared bowls of ramen. "Did you play sports growing up?" Megumi asks. Ryan nods. "I played baseball as a kid. Then I got really into mountain biking, snowboarding and martial arts." Megumi looks impressed, "Wow. Martial Arts? Like Judo?" Ryan nods. "Jiu Jitsu and Karate. Do you know Jiu Jitsu?" She nods, "My brother trained Judo and Jiu Jitsu a lot when we were kids." He smiles, "Did you do ever do martial arts?" She chuckles, "Only with what my brother taught me at home. And I had to go watch him in class, and when he competed." Ryan is intrigued, "Did you like it?" She laughs heartily, "I was bored out of my mind." They both laugh. Ryan shifts the conversation back to her, "How about you? Did you ever play sports?" She nods, "I golfed. Have you ever golfed?" Ryan nods, "Yeah, a couple of times. I was horrible." She laughs, "I teach you how to golf, and you teach me snowboarding. Deal?" He nods, "Deal." They look deeply into each others eyes and the rest of the world fades away.

Chapter Thirty-One

Let's go back to bed!

Ryan and Megumi burst through the doors of her luxurious penthouse, their laughter filling the spacious living area. She playfully attempts to tickle him, her fingers dancing alongside his ribs. Ryan's eyes sparkle with a childlike energy, his laughter mingling with hers in a melody of shared joy. Their coats are swiftly discarded in the rush of their game, falling haphazardly onto the floor. The chase is on. Megumi takes off towards the bedroom, her laughter trailing behind her like a whimsical comet tail. Ryan is hot on her heels, the thrill of the chase igniting a playful light within him. The world outside the penthouse fades into oblivion as they lose themselves in this shared moment, a testament to their blossoming relationship. Their laughter continues to echo in the room, punctuated by playful banter and shared glances. The outside world fades, and for a moment, it's just the two of them, lost in their world of laughter and love.

She runs and jumps onto the bed. She looks at him playfully, "Come and get me!" He smiles, runs over to the bed and lays down next to her. She rolls over and looks at him playfully, "I just wanted to get you back into bed. You're in trouble now." She says with a playful gleam in her eyes. He shakes his head, "You're in big trouble now.." She laughs, he continues, "I'm a twenty-fifth degree black belt in tickle Jiu Jitsu." She feigns an impressed look. "You don't believe me?" he teases. She shakes her head, "Prove it!" He starts to tickle her and they laugh hysterically.

Neither have ever felt this comfortable, happy or fulfilled in their entire lives.

CHAPTER THIRTY-TWO

Sweet & Sour

Megumi walked into the meeting room, a bubbly energy radiating from her that was uncharacteristic of her typical stoicism. Ryan's heart skipped a beat as he watched her stride in, her eyes sparkling with an infectious joy. As she took her seat across from him, he could almost feel the happy energy she emanated, warming him like a sunbeam.

Jun, their charismatic marketing leader, initiated the meeting with a smile directed at Megumi. This smiling Megumi was a pleasant surprise to everyone in the room. Jun, with his inborn charm, set the rhythm of the meeting in sync with Megumi's upbeat attitude, making the usually strenuous session feel like a breeze. Their relationship was not public, so Ryan tried hard to hide his affection for their CEO.

The mood in the meeting room was noticeably lighter. Laughter punctuated the discussion of sales figures and marketing strategies, and even the most serious topics were tackled with an underlying sense of optimism. Megumi's happiness was infectious, transforming a dull meeting into a motivating brainstorming session. It was a testament to the power of happiness and its ability to change not just a person, but an entire room.

Completely oblivious to the underlying romantic relationship between Ryan and Megumi, the marketing team found themselves captivated by the positive shift in the dynamics of their workplace. They noticed an increased sense of camaraderie, an upsurge in creative ideas, and a renewed level of commitment, but they attributed it all to the newfound exuberance of their usually reserved CEO. Little did they know that the magic that was transforming the office atmosphere was the blossoming love between the two.

As the meeting neared its conclusion, Jun took the reins, seamlessly transitioning into the next steps of executing the campaign. His voice echoed through the room with authority and clarity, capturing the team's attention - all except Megumi. Her gaze, usually attentive and focused, strayed from Jun to settle on Ryan. Eyes shimmering with unspoken emotion, she watched him as he sat engrossed, his focus intent on Jun's words. However, Mika, the ever-observant brand strategist, noticed the fleeting exchange. A flicker of realization dawned on her face as she began to piece together the dynamic between Megumi and Ryan. The tiny office romance was no longer a well-kept secret - at least not from Mika.

As the meeting drew to a close, the team, now buzzing with energy and ideas, began to disperse. Megumi was the first to rise, her aura radiating an infectious level of happiness. She left the room with an air of satisfaction, followed by the others, until the bustling office was reduced to just two individuals - Ryan and Mika.

Jun, the effective leader he was, wrapped up his notes and exited the office, leaving behind a silence that only amplified the anticipation in the air. Mika turned towards Ryan, a wily smile tugging at the corners of her lips. "Have you noticed how much happier Megumi seems these days?" she asked, her gaze fixed on him, searching for a reaction.

Ryan, keeping his composure, merely shrugged, feigning ignorance. "Yeah, I guess so?" he responded, his face a mask of innocence. Mika's smile widened, her intrigue piqued by Ryan's nonchalant facade. The secret might not have been as well-hidden as they had thought.

As the clock struck eight, the office was bathed in the gentle silence. The usual humdrum had drawn to a close, and the once lively workspace stood in stark contrast, mostly deserted with only a few stragglers wrapping up their day's work. Ryan was one of them. Nestled in his office, he was engrossed in his work when the door creaked open, and Megumi walked in, shutting the door behind her. She sauntered over to him, her eyes sparkling with a hint of playfulness.

Leaning casually against his desk, she asked nonchalantly, "Free for dinner?" His face lit up with a smile, a clear indication of his acceptance. He nodded, adding, "Definitely" With a knowing smile, she suggested, "I'll leave first? You follow a few minutes later. So people don't talk." Ryan chuckled at her forethought, and they both knew their secret was safe, at least for now. Megumi flashes him a warm smile before walking from the office. His eyes are fixated on her as she leaves.

Ryan is sitting at his desk, his eyes watching the hallway for Megumi to pass by. Megumi appears, and steals a wry smile in at Ryan. Ryan smiles back. His smile fades quickly as he sees Mika approach Megumi. What looks like small talk from Mika feels much more ominous now. Ryan knows that Mika is figuring things out.

A few minutes have passed and Ryan throws his laptop bag over his shoulder. He flips out the lights as he closes his door behind him.

He makes his way down the hall towards the elevator and his heart skips a beat as he sees Megumi talking with Mika. To an outsider, the conversation looks harmless - a subordinate talking with her CEO. To Ryan, it feels much more dangerous and manipulative. As Ryan approaches, Mika looks up to him, "Done for the night?" she smiles. Ryan smiles, trying to appear casual, "Yep, you?" She nods. Ryan looks over to Megumi and nods politely. The elevator door opens, Ryan nods for Megumi and Mika to enter. They do, and he files in last.

Inside of the elevator, Mika and Megumi continue their small talk. Ryan stands silently. After what feels like and eternity, the elevator finally reaches the ground floor. The doors open and the three step out and make their way through the lobby and out toward the busy street. As they exit the building, Mika looks over to Ryan playfully, "Want to go get some food? I know of a good Thai place nearby?" Mika shoots a quick look to Megumi, "You too?" Mika looks back to Ryan, who looks awkward, "Uh, no, thank you. I already have plans." Mika smiles, "Big date?" Ryan shakes his head, "No, no. Just meeting up with a buddy over in Shibuya." Mika turns to Megumi, "How about you? Dinner?" Megumi smiles politely, trying to hide her sudden disdain for the young and pretty girl who is trying to steal Ryan's attention, "I have to get home. Thank you though for the kind invitation. Some other time?" Ryan feels the shift in mood, "Alright, hope you both have a great night." He leaves.

As Ryan trudges away, a battle rages within him. He yearns to spin around, confront Mika outright, and proclaim to the world that the one he truly yearns for is Megumi. He imagines himself declaring, with no room for doubt, that he has no intention of ever sharing a meal with her. Yet, these words remain trapped within him, choking him, every step he takes. The images of them together - Megumi, his love, and Mika, the intruder - replayed in his mind, stirring a typhoon of emotions. But he swallows down his feelings, his words, his truth. He can't let them out, not yet. The world wasn't ready for his confession.

CHAPTER THIRTY-THREE
Unspoken

An hour had swept by since they had left the office, the episode with Mika still loomed like an unwelcomed guest. The evening found Ryan and Megumi nestled in a small, modern cafe, its ambient lighting casting a soft, warm glow on their faces. A jazz melody was playing softly in the background, mingling with the low hum of conversations.

Megumi sat across from Ryan, stirring her coffee absently, her gaze fixed on the swirling dark liquid. Her mind was a whirlpool of thoughts, her heart, a maelstrom of emotions. Ryan, on the other hand, was trying to be the comforting presence he believed she needed. He reached across the table, gently covering her hand with his. His eyes, filled with unspoken affection, bore into hers.

"Hey," He offered a gentle smile, "You've been quiet. Everything okay?" He suggested, hoping to steer her thoughts away from Mika and their recent encounter. His voice was soft, tender - a stark contrast to the tumultuous feelings that threatened to spill from his heart. Unbeknownst to both, they sat there, under the dim café lights, each battling their own silent wars, their words remaining unspoken, their feelings untouched. Megumi looks up momentarily and back to her coffee, "I'm okay. You?" He nods, "Yeah, I'm okay." Megumi still looking down. Ryan can't hold it any longer, "Actually no, I am not okay." Megumi looks up, puzzled. Ryan continues, "I feel like you're upset." She shakes her head, "I'm just a bit tired. Long day." He nods, "Yeah, me too. Want to get this to go? Go back to my place?" His words hang in the air. Megumi still not looking up, "That's a good idea. We should have them pack this up. But maybe tonight, we just take a break?" Ryan gets a sinking feeling, "Take a break?" Still not looking up, she nods, "Maybe you just go back to your place, and I go back to mine?" Her words hit him like a direct punch to the gut.

Ryan gathers his thoughts. The idea of being away from Megumi, even just for one night feels torturous. He needs her like he needs air. Just as he puts together his response, the server approaches with their food. Megumi looks up to the server, trying to force a polite smile as she fights back tears of her own, "Can you please pack this to go? Two separate bags please?" The server reads the tension between Ryan and Megumi and he nods, "Of course." He leaves with the food. Ryan sits, frozen. His moment has passed.

Ryan and Megumi are standing outside of the restaurant. They stand beside each other, but the feel a world apart. The fact that each are holding a plastic, to-go bag of food highlights the despair of unfinished business and words unspoken. Megumi holds up her hand to hail a taxi cab. A cab pulls over to the curb and the driver gets out, comes around and opens the door. This is Ryan's chance to right the wrongs, to say the things that need to be said, and hopefully get things back on track.

Before Megumi can get into the cab, Ryan walks to the driver, quickly pulls out 300 yen and hands it to the driver, "My apologies, we didn't need the car after all. Please take this for your trouble." The driver, a stern looking man in his forties, just looks at Ryan. Ryan extends the cash. The driver looks over to Megumi, "It's the lady's cab." Ryan shakes his head, "No, we don't need it. My apologies." The driver looks to Megumi, as she fights back tears. The cab driver persists, "Ma'am, your car?" Ryan is visibly angry, his words now frightening threatening, "I told you. Take this cash, with my apologies... and please... get the fuck out of here. Now." The cab driver backs down, taking the cash, "Have a good night." His words are insincere. Ryan steps in, slams the cab door shut and the driver gets in and drives away. Ryan turns his full attention back to Megumi. She looks at him with a mix of shock and relief.

"I know what's upsetting you. It's Mika. That little shit Mika." Ryan says, holding nothing back. Megumi starts to interject but Ryan cuts her off cold, "So let me be really clear with you. I have never liked her, never been attracted to her, not one bit. You get in that car, you go back to your place, and you may as well drive a sword through my heart. The idea of being away from you, even for one night.. it would kill me."

Tears are now streaming down Megumi's face, "She's younger than me. She's very pretty. And she's not the only one. All of the girls in the office want your attention. I hear them talking."

Ryan shakes his head, "And what are they saying? I have never paid attention to any of them. It's only been you. It's always been you. Just you."

Megumi's eyes are filled with tears. She gathers herself, "Have you ever lost anyone Ryan?"

Ryan doesn't know how to answer. Megumi continues, "This is all new to me. I can't lose you." Ryan shakes his head, a comforting smile come across his face. He pulls her close, "I love you. I have never loved anyone like I love you. I would gladly lay down in front of a train before I would ever let you get hurt."

Megumi pulls away gently to look into Ryan's eyes for what feels like an eternity, "It's not just Mika. You're still married. What if you change your mind and go back to America? And your wife? What happens to me then?"

Ryan smiles slightly, "My divorce is final. I just have to go back to Los Angeles to sign the papers. I wasn't saying anything because I didn't want to bring it up. By the way can I take a few vacation days to go sign the papers?" He chuckles.

Mika is in disbelief, "It's finalized?" He nods with a smile on his face, "I found out earlier today. I was going to tell you tonight."

She is just standing there trying to reconcile her emotions. Ryan continues, "My divorce is final. It's over. Even if you dump me tonight. Even if you never talk to me again.. I will stay single. There is nobody else I want. If you need time.. truly need time and space, I will give it to you. I would wait for you forever. As long as it takes."

They look deeply into each other's eyes. The icy wall that was between them before has fully melted. Megumi smiles, "Your divorce is final?" Ryan nods. Megumi smiles, "Marry me?" Without a moment of hesitation Ryan replies, "Yes." Megumi smiles, "I know I sound crazy.." Ryan shakes his head, "No, you don't. As a matter of fact..." He slips his fitness ring off of his right hand index finger and he gets down on one knee. He holds it up to Megumi, "Megumi Sato, I want to marry you. Would you please do me the honor of marrying me? You will make me the happiest man in the entire world."

A small group of passersby have noticed the interaction and stopped to watch. Ryan and Megumi are oblivious to the onlookers. Megumi breaks out into a broad smile and nods yes, her heart and eyes filled with pure joy. The moment she said "Yes" the passersby broke out into applause. Ryan and Megumi look over to them. Ryan gets up from his knee and slips the ring onto her tiny and delicately manicured hand. The ring is obviously too big and they share a chuckle. Ryan jokes, "I will get you a real ring of course.. and one that fits." She smiles, "I'm keeping this one too." He grins, "Of course."

The crowd starts to disperse. Ryan holds up his bag of food, "I'm starving. Want to go home and heat these up?" She smiles and nods yes.

Chapter Thirty-Four

Cleaning Day

The ordinary hum of the office surrounded Mika as she sat at her desk, immersed in her work. Under the soft glow of her desk lamp, she sifted through the pile of documents that seemed to have grown exponentially since morning. The sound of clicking keys and occasional ringing phones served as a symphony of productivity, a shared song of diligence and focus.

Suddenly, the rhythm was interrupted. The HR manager, a tall figure in a crisp suit, approached her desk. His presence was always a bit intimidating, not because of his size, but because his visits usually brought change - a change in responsibilities, a change in teams, sometimes even a change in the office location. As he drew nearer, Mika could feel her heartbeat quicken, echoing the silent question, *What now?*

The HR manager paused before Mika's desk, his gaze steady and unreadable. "Mika, could you join me in my office please?" he asked, his tone as formal as his attire. Surprise and intrigue flickered across Mika's face, replacing the focused expression she had moments ago. She nodded, quickly saving her work and locking her computer. As she rose from her chair, she couldn't help but wonder what this impromptu office meeting could mean.

In the HR manager's office, an air of solemnity hung heavy. He motioned for Mika to take a seat across from his desk. There was a moment of silence before he finally spoke. "Mika, I'll get straight to the point," he began, his voice carrying a regretful tone. "The company has decided to terminate your contract."

The words hung in the air like a crushing weight. Mika was taken aback. Anger and confusion clouded her features. "What?" she exclaimed. "Why? I don't understand. I've been meeting all my targets, haven't I?" Her mind was racing, grappling with this sudden, unforeseen turn of events. She felt a surge of resentment, blindsided by this decision and uncertain about her future. The HR manager remained silent, offering no further explanation. This left Mika questioning her worth and, more importantly, what her next steps would be.

"Can you tell me why?" Mika questioned, her voice barely above a whisper. She searched the HR manager's face for any hint of empathy or understanding, but all she found was a stony, unreadable expression. The silence between them was deafening, amplifying the significance of each passing second.

The HR manager leaned back in his chair, his gaze never leaving Mika. "I'm afraid I can't provide more details, Mika," he responded, his tone disappointingly cold. "The decision is final. Today will be your last day with us."

Mika felt a lump in her throat. The walls of the office seemed to close in on her, the reality of the situation sinking in fully. It was over. She was being terminated, left to confront an uncertain future with no explanation as to why.

Ryan was engrossed in his work when he noticed a figure standing in the doorway. It was Mika, clutching a box filled with her personal belongings. Her eyes were teary, but her posture was firm.

"Mika, what's going on?" Ryan asked, confusion etched on his face.

"I've been let go," Mika stuttered, her gaze locked with Ryan's, "Can you tell me why?."

Ryan was taken aback by the news. "I...I have no idea, Mika." His voice was filled with genuine surprise, "I'm just as blindsided as you are."

Just then, Jun, approached Mika. He was always respectful and understanding, but today, he wore a somber expression that mirrored the gloomy atmosphere of the office.

"Excuse me, Mika, but you should probably go," Jun suggested politely, gesturing toward the exit. Mika, in a daze, nodded and quietly made her way out of the office.

After Mika's departure, Jun walked past the glass-paneled office of Megumi. He gave her a silent nod, their understood language in these challenging situations. Megumi, from behind her desk, flashed Jun an appreciative smile in return. She called in a favor and he executed it with a cold efficiency.

CHAPTER THIRTY-FIVE

Endings and Beginnings

The evening found Ryan seated at an ornately carved wooden dining table, set against the backdrop of panoramic city views from Megumi's penthouse. The room was filled with the rich aroma of homemade food. A sumptuous spread lay before him -- a steaming bowl of miso soup, a platter of sushi, and a plate of tempura vegetables.

Megumi, moving seamlessly from CEO to housewife, poured them both a glass of aged sake. She was elegantly dressed in black yoga pants and a soft pink hoodie, her dark hair pinned up, revealing the graceful curve of her neck. Ryan was staring at her and she noticed, "Everything okay?" she asked. Ryan nods, "You get more beautiful every time I see you." She smiles and their eyes lock in a passionate, yet wordless exchange.

Ryan breaks the silence, "I booked my flight back to LA. I am leaving Thursday night." Megumi makes a pouty face, "How long are you gone?" Ryan raises his eyebrows and takes a deep breath, "Two maybe three days. Depends on how fast it all gets signed off and processed. Then, I am free and we can start our life together."

Something in this strikes a chord within her. She shoots him a seductive look as she stands from the table. She extends her hand, half offering, half commanding, "Come with me." He takes her hand and she leads him from the room.

They make their way from the dining room to the bedroom. Once in the bedroom she removes her hoodie. She starts to unbutton Ryan's shirt as she whispers sweetly in his ear, "I want to give you a little something to remember me by when you are in LA.."

Ryan chuckles as she continues to unbutton his beautifully pressed dress shirt, "Remember you? You're all I ever think about." She continues, "Exactly as it should be."

Far below the penthouse, cars and people pulse through the crowded city streets, oblivious to the passionate encounter taking place high above.

CHAPTER THIRTY-SIX

Los Angeles

Ryan stood, somewhat disoriented, amid the hustle and bustle of Haneda Airport. The bright lights, the ceaseless hum of conversations in multiple languages, and the rhythmic announcement of departures and arrivals were all strangely comforting. His luggage was checked, and he clutched his boarding pass in hand. The destination read "Los Angeles".

He navigated through the labyrinthine structure of the enormous airport, his mind preoccupied with thoughts of Megumi. Each step he took felt like a step away from her, but he knew it was necessary for them to be together in the long run.

Arriving at the gate, he found a quiet corner and sat down, staring out of the vast glass window. Outside, the planes awaited their missions, gleaming under the floodlights. He pulled out his phone to check the time, then instinctively opened the gallery, his eyes drawn to the latest picture of Megumi.

As he waited for his flight, the reality of the distance he was about to put between them started to sink in. He held his phone close, his finger tracing the contours of her face on the screen. The words echoed in his mind, "Exactly as it should be."

With a deep breath, he typed a simple yet powerful message, "I love you", and hit send. His heart pounded in anxious anticipation. Seconds later, his phone buzzed, indicating an incoming call. Megumi's name flashed across the screen. He swiftly swiped to answer, instantly hearing her soft voice. "Ryan," she said, her voice trembling slightly, "Have a safe flight. I'm going to miss you so much." Her words, although filled with sadness, carried an underlying warmth that comforted him, reinforcing that their love was strong enough to weather the distance that would soon separate them. Ryan comforts her, "I am going to miss you even more. I forgot to ask, do you want me to get you anything while I am in LA?" She chuckles, "Yes, you. I want you. All to myself for the rest of my life. Just get divorced, and then come back to me." He smiles as he looks around at the others waiting at the gate, "You already have that. You always have." With that, he tells her to have a good rest of her night and hangs up.

The flight begins boarding. Ryan picks up his bag and makes his way over to get in line. From the looks of it, there are not many passengers making the trip. He smiles. This trip seems to be off to a great start.

Ryan was jolted from his sleep by the overhead announcement; they were landing in Los Angeles in twenty minutes. His eyes blinked open, sleep still clinging to the edges of his vision as he tried to re-orient himself in the dim cabin lighting. His heart pounded in his chest; the reality of the situation was starting to set in. An instinctive reaction made him reach out to lift the window shade, squinting as the sunlight flooded in. Down below, the city sprawled out, a vast expanse of concrete, buildings, and life far removed from his own. He took a moment to take in the sight, the city of Los Angeles stretching out beneath him, a new chapter waiting to unfold.

He once called Los Angeles home. He was born and raised here. Now it feels strangely foreign to him.

Bags in hand, Ryan navigates his way through the bustling crowd. Upon reaching the curb, he raises an arm, hailing a taxi cab. The cab pulls up swiftly, and he slides into the comfort of its backseat, relishing in the temporary solitude. He pulls out his phone, checking the clock - it displays the time in Tokyo. Opening his messages, he finds two new texts waiting for him; one from Megumi, expressing her love, and another from Allie, inquiring about his arrival time. He swiftly replies to Megumi, reassuring her of his safe arrival and punctuating his message with a heartfelt emoji. His fingers dance across the screen as he sends another message, this one directed at Allie. His message is simple – he has arrived safely and will update her once he reaches his hotel.

As the taxi drives through the opulence of Beverly Hills, Ryan gazes out of the window, watching the play of sunlight on pristine white walls and the glint of luxury cars parked in driveways. He is jolted out of his reverie as the taxi pulls up in front of the grand facade of the Beverly Wilshire Hotel. He pays the driver, his heart beating in anticipation as he picks up his bags and steps out of the cab. The grandeur of the Beverly Wilshire Hotel takes his breath away. He stands for a moment, taking in the sight of the stunning lobby and the busy hustle and bustle within. Gathering his composure, he walks forward, pushing open the grand double doors and steps into the cool, elegant lobby of the hotel. With each step, the reality of his new journey gets etched deeper into his heart. As he passes through the lobby, the ghosts of yesteryear play in his mind. He looks over at the bar, where just a year ago, Ryan and his friends used to frequent, enjoying after dinner drinks and soaking in the nightlife. It brings back memories of he and Allie dancing on New Year's Eve and shopping across the street on Rodeo Drive.

Ryan snaps out of his reverie and approaches the check-in desk. Jet lag and outright fatigue are hitting him hard. He checks in to his hotel, gets his room key and makes his way over to the elevators.

The door to his room swings open and Ryan enters. As he makes his way over to the closet, he sets his bag down and flops down on the bed. His cell phone vibrates with an incoming call. He sees that it's Allie calling him. He answers.

"Hey Allie," Ryan manages to greet, stifling a yawn, "What's up?"

"Perfect timing, Ryan," Allie's voice sounds excited over the phone. "I'm actually already at the hotel. How about we catch up? Meet me at the hotel bar?"

Ryan sits up at the mention of the bar, a wave of nostalgia washing over him. "Sure, Allie. I'll see you there in a few," he replies, pushing off the fatigue. He hangs up, gets up from the bed, and starts to freshen up for the unexpected meet-up downstairs.

Ryan enters the bar area of the luxurious hotel. Instantly, his eyes lock in on Allie. Dressed to perfection and wearing a smile. He walks over, trying to hide how nice it is to see her. He needs to stay focused on the task at hand. Sign the divorce papers and get back to Megumi.

Allie stands up as Ryan approaches, it's so awkward. Technically they are man and wife, but it's more like two strangers being forced into a blind date. "Let's grab a table." Ryan asks. Allie nods yes and they make their way over to an empty table.

Allie looks around, "I love this place. So many good times." Ryan nods calmly, "True. Lots of good times. Do you have the papers?" Visibly disappointed, she pulls the papers out of her bag and sets them on the table in front of him, "Here you go."

Ryan starts shuffling through the papers, reviewing line by line. As Ryan studies the papers, Rodrigo, a server and old friend of Ryan and Allie's approaches, "I see it but I don't believe it! Damn, how are you guys? It's been forever." Ryan smiles heartily, "Oh man, so good to see you too." Rodrigo, still in disbelief, continues, "What can I get you?" Ryan nods, "Diet Coke?" Rodrigo looks to Allie. Allie replies, "Vodka tonic." Rodrigo takes note of both orders and looks back to Ryan, "I heard you guys moved to Tokyo? How long are you in town for? We should get together?"

Ryan replies, "Just a couple of days. Pretty quick turnaround." Rodrigo is impressed. Rodrigo looks to Allie, "How is Tokyo? Is it amazing?" She just flashes an awkward smile, "Ryan is the only one who went. I think he likes it?" She looks over at Ryan with an awkward grin. Rodrigo nods before leaving to get their drinks. As soon as he is out of earshot, Allie looks to Ryan, "So.. I take it you don't want to try to fix things.. like you said?" Ryan does not even look up, "There was a time when that was all I wanted. But not anymore."

Allie is a bitch. She is used to getting whatever she wants from anybody she comes across. However, things are different now. She overplayed her hand and Ryan has moved on. She feels it and she doesn't like it.

Ryan signs the papers and looks to her, "This is my copy?" She just nods. Ryan continues, "You're going to get these filed? Or would you like me to?" Allie is surprised at Ryan's transformation. When he left for Tokyo, he was her puppet. Now he is like a completely different person. Reluctantly she replies, "I can get them filed."

Ryan nods, "Awesome. Thank you." Casually, Ryan pulls some cash out of his wallet and puts it on the table, "I need to take off, let me get the drinks." He stands up and readies to walk away. Allie is taken off guard, "The drinks aren't even here yet?" He nods, "I need to get some sleep." She nods and he continues, "Look, I am really sorry that things didn't work out with us. We are just two different people. I really hope that you find what you are looking for. Please tell Rodrigo it was good seeing him." With that, he walks away without looking back.

Upon entering his room, he quickly retrieves his phone, sending a succinct text to Megumi, "Divorce finalized. I'm free! I cannot wait to spend the rest of my life with you." The message is simple, yet its implications are profound; it's an end and a beginning. As the last vestiges of his old life slip away, so too does he slip out of his clothes, stepping into the warm embrace of the shower. The water cascades down, washing away the remnants of the evening, and he finally feels a sense of closure. This chapter of his life has ended, allowing a new one to begin.

Ryan makes his way from the shower to the closet where he pulls a large and extremely comfortable bathrobe from the hanger. He slips it on. He finally feels free and happy. Everything is perfect in his world now.

He makes his way over to the bed. It's made for two, and this makes him miss Megumi even more. He puts the phone on the bed beside him and closes his eyes. He should be comfortable. The divorce is complete, the shower was soothing and this bed, let's just say it's beyond comfortable. He closes his eyes, but he cannot sleep. He misses Megumi in a way he never before imagined. Just then his phone rings. Quickly he answers, "Hey, how are you?" He listens, "I'm great. It's done. She had the papers and we both signed." Just then, the doorbell to the suite sounded.

"Damn. One second. I ordered some food when I first got here.. hold on, okay?" He gets up from the bed, still with the phone to his ear and he opens the door.

Allie is standing in the hallway. She notices Ryan on the phone, but she proceeds, "Can we talk?" Ryan is dumbfounded. He looks at Allie, and speaks into the phone, "Let me call you right back. Two minutes." He ends the call and looks to Allie, "What's up?"

Allie sighs deeply, "Can I come in?" Ryan is hesitant. She persists,

"Ryan, we were married. Now it's over. The least you can do is let me in so we can talk." With that, she doesn't wait for a reply. She walks in and looks around.

It's clear that Ryan does not want her here. "What's up? He asks. She makes her way over to the bed and sits down. Ryan is still standing, clutching the phone. He cannot wait to call Megumi back. Allie continues, "You've changed." Ryan nods, "You have too."

Allie stands up and pulls herself in close to Ryan, "I like this new you. Maybe we ended things too quickly? Maybe I can change your mind?" She is trying her seductive best. He has never been able to resist her. This time everything feels different. Ryan steps back away from her. She makes an angry face.

"You fly fourteen hours to come here. You sign the papers and you just walk away? Just like that? Why don't you try to get to know me again? I think you will like it?" She gives him her most manipulatively sweet smile as she tries to pull in close again. Again, Ryan backs away.

Ryan's mind is racing. Did Megumi hear Allie's voice? He needed to call Megumi back and he needed to call her back now. Ryan shakes his head, "We are done. I need you to leave. There is nothing left to say... or do." He walks over to the door and opens it.

She stands, looking at Ryan as he holds the door open. Anger and shock on her face. After what feels like an eternity she makes her way to the door. She turns to face him again, but he is already shutting the door.

That would be the last time he would ever see Allie again.

As soon as the door clicks shut behind Allie, Ryan dives for his phone. His hands are shaking slightly as he navigates to his recent calls and dials Megumi's number. The line rings once, twice, before she picks up. "Hello?" Her voice drifts from the speaker, sounding cool and distant, a stark contrast to their usual warm conversations. "Megumi,"

Ryan begins, struggling to keep his voice steady, "Everything okay?"

There's a pause on the other end of the line, and then Megumi's voice returns, quieter now, "Yes, Ryan. Everything's fine." Her assurance doesn't sit well with him; it lacks the usual vivacity that is distinctively Megumi. His chest tightens, an unsettling feeling creeping into his gut. "Megumi," Ryan insists, "You don't sound like yourself. Did you hear someone else on the line? Did you hear Allie?" Another pause, longer this time, followed by a soft sigh. "Yes, I heard her," Megumi confesses, her voice barely a whisper. Ryan's heart sinks. He had hoped he was wrong. Now, with the truth hanging in the air between them, a heavy silence sets in. The call ends abruptly, leaving Ryan in a pool of worry and unease, a stark contrast to the relief he felt moments ago.

Ryan takes a deep breath, steadying himself before he speaks again. "Megumi," he starts, "I need you to believe me. I signed the papers, I got up, and I left. Allie followed me to my room, but I made her leave." His voice wavers, betraying a hint of emotion. There's a pause on the other end of the line, then a light sigh. "Ryan. I believe you," Megumi says. Her voice is still quiet, but there's a warmth there now, a thread of trust weaving its way back into their conversation. Ryan feels the weight lift from his shoulders. They talk a bit more, their conversation flowing back into familiar patterns, the rhythm of their friendship returning to its normal cadence.

"Listen, Megumi," Ryan says, his voice firm now, "I need you to know something important. I love you. I love you and only you. I promise, my loyalty to you is unwavering." His words hang in the air, a testament to his sincerity. There's another pause, then a soft laugh from Megumi, her tone brightening. "Ryan," she responds, "I never doubted you. I know you wouldn't do anything to hurt us. I love you too." The ease returns to their conversation, their bond stronger than before. The call ends on a lighter note, their relationship solidified in the face of adversity.

As the call ends, Ryan places his phone down and sinks into the bed, staring blankly at the ceiling. His mind is a whirlwind of thoughts, a tumultuous storm fueled by the day's events and his confession. Despite the persistent thrum of jet lag and exhaustion from the long flight, sleep eludes him, his mind too active to succumb to rest.

With a sigh, he pushes himself up, slips on his shoes and grabs his room key and heads for the door. He exits the room and makes his way over to the elevators in the poshly decorated hallway.

Stepping out into the lively atmosphere of Santa Monica's Third Street Promenade, Ryan finds himself drawn to a small specialty store nestled among the bustling shops. The store is unique, its charm evident in the variety of trinkets and souvenirs representative of the local culture. His eyes are drawn to a particular item, a small stuffed animal perched atop a display, a Shiba Inu dog adorned with a little sweater emblazoned with the words "Santa Monica, California, USA". He picks it up, the soft material warm in his hands, and a smile tugs at his lips. He imagines Megumi's surprise and delight upon seeing this cute little token. Ryan proceeds to the counter, ready to pay for the stuffed dog, his heart light with anticipation of the joy it will bring.

With the stuffed animal safely tucked away in his bag, Ryan finally feels the sense of completion he's been longing for. He retreats from the vibrant energy of the Promenade, making his way back to the tranquility of his hotel room. Once there, he wastes no time in booking his return flight to Tokyo, the familiar process offering a comforting semblance of normalcy amidst the day's whirlwind events. Flight secured, exhaustion finally overtakes him. He sinks into the plush hotel bed, the anticipation of his return journey home and the joy his gift will bring acting as a soothing lullaby. Sleep, previously elusive, now greets him like a long-lost friend, and he succumbs willingly, knowing tomorrow's journey brings him closer to sharing his Californian souvenir with Megumi.

CHAPTER THIRTY-SEVEN
Found and Lost

The sun had barely risen, its tentative rays attempting to penetrate the blinds of Megumi's office. It was 8 am and the day was just beginning. As the city outside her window was slowly awakening, so was Megumi's workday. Settled comfortably in her chair, she was engrossed in her tasks when her phone buzzed. Ryan's name lit up her screen, instantly bringing a soft smile to her face.

"Flight 287, LAX to Haneda," Ryan's voice echoed from the other side of the call. Megumi swiftly echoed the information, her pen dancing on her notepad, etching the words "287 LAX Haneda". He spoke with an undercurrent of excitement, "I'll be leaving in three hours, it was the first one I could get."

His words sent a wave of anticipation through her. The thought of seeing him soon, of being in his arms, made her heart flutter. "I can't wait to hold you in my arms," he confessed, his voice low and filled with emotion.

A warm smile spread across her face as she responded, her words teeming with love, "I love you, Ryan." With those words hanging in the air, they ended the call, each lost in their thoughts of their impending reunion.

As the meeting with the various department heads carried on, Megumi's attention seemed to be elsewhere. She sat at the head of the conference table, her eyes occasionally drifting from the figures and charts being presented to the screen of her phone, shimmering with time. Each passing minute brought Ryan closer to her, and this thought alone filled her with a sense of elation that superseded the pressing matters being discussed in the room. In her mind, she painted vivid images of Ryan at the airport, his luggage in tow, a smiling face obscured behind the boarding pass. The mental picture of him stepping onto the flight that would bring him back to her was enough to make her heart skip a beat. For Megumi, the joy of their impending reunion was a far more compelling reality than the droning voices that echoed around the conference room.

As the hands of the clock continued to move inexorably forward, Megumi found herself glancing at her phone yet again. The glowing digits displayed the passing time, their relentless march both a reassurance and a torment. She did a quick mental calculation and a sense of relief washed over her. *"Okay, Ryan should be in the air by now,"* she thought to herself. She envisioned the plane cutting through the clouds, carrying him across the ocean towards her. This thought brought a smile to her face, a bright spot of joy that momentarily eclipsed the tedious meeting surrounding her.

The last to present was the Human Resources Manager, a pretty and very refined Japanese lady in her late forties. Her given name is also Megumi, but everyone knows her as Linda. As she began to relay the recent personnel updates, her normally crisp, business-like tone was absent. She faltered mid-sentence, her eyes drawn to the television screen mounted on the wall. The room fell eerily silent as the live news report came into focus. A plane crash. Just outside of Los Angeles. The television volume was low, but the news anchor's voice seemed to echo around the room, the words carrying a weight heavy enough to suck the air out of the room. Linda, still standing, stopped her presentation in mid sentence. Her eyes were drawn to the television. She murmured "Wow." Her eyes wide. Megumi followed her gaze, and looked up at the screen just as the news anchor delivered a line she would never forget, "Flight 287, Los Angeles destined for Tokyo crashed shortly after takeoff. Confirmed no survivors."

The room was frozen in a tableau of shock and disbelief, the tragic news washing over them like a chilling wave. Each pair of eyes was glued to the screen, but none could fathom the depth of despair that had just gripped Megumi. Ryan, her Ryan, was on that flight. The love of her life, the man she was eagerly waiting to embrace, was now lost forever in a cruel twist of fate. The truth felt like a merciless whip, lashing her reality and shattering it into a million fragments. This was her private nightmare and in the room full of people, she was completely alone. The anguish seemed to strangle her, a silent scream lodged in her throat. If this was a dream, it was time to wake up. But the hollow reality stared at her from the screen, merciless and real.

Megumi's eyes were frozen on the television screen. The vibrant colors of the news report seemed to dull into an insipid monotone. The words "No survivors" echoed in her head, each syllable a piercing stab of reality. She felt like she was drowning in a sea of white noise, the world around her becoming a blur. Her heartbeat was loud in her ears, drowning out the stunned silence of the room. The faces around her were a mix of shock and sympathy, but all she could focus on was the piercing pain in her chest. It felt as if her heart had been ripped out and all she was left with was a hollow emptiness. She felt weak, her knees buckling under the weight of the unbearable truth. As the room began to sway, the last thing she saw was the haunting image of the burning plane wreckage on the television screen.

With an immense effort, Megumi stood up, her face a mask of professionalism, betraying no hint of the ocean of sorrow and loss just beneath. "I think we've covered everything we need to for today's meeting. Let's convene again next week," she said, her voice remarkably steady. No one in the room knew about the secret she and Ryan had shared, their plans of a life together, dreams of marriage that now lay in tatters. To them, it was just another news report. A shocking one, but plane crashes happen from time to time. To her, it was her world, her life that went down in flames.

She forced a smile and left the meeting room. She had to get back to her office, close the door and seal herself in so she could process this horrible and shocking news. As Megumi left so abruptly, her colleagues looked around. They were surprised at the quick end to the meeting, but nobody said a word. One by one, they stood up and filed out, the news report still playing quietly on the television.

Once inside her office, Megumi wasted no time before she was reaching for her phone, dialing Ryan's number in a desperate hope. *There has to be a mistake*, she thought to herself, her fingers trembling as they moved over the screen, *He can't be gone just like that*. The phone rang, a shrill sound in the otherwise silent room. It rang and rang, only to be answered by his voicemail. The sound of his voice, a sound she once found comfort in, now felt like a sharp, painful reminder of what she had lost. His cheerful greeting echoed in the room, but all she felt was an overwhelming sense of loss, a harsh reality that he really was gone.

Feeling a mixture of desperation and denial, Megumi dialed again. The same, familiar ringtone filled the room, a sound that now seemed to echo the silence of her heart. She held her breath, every ring a hope, a plea, a prayer. "Pick up, pick up," she muttered under her breath, her voice barely above a whisper. Yet, the universe remained deaf to her pleas. Once again, it was his voicemail that answered. His voice, lively and warm, played out the same recorded message. The words "Sorry, I can't come to the phone right now..." bore into her, each syllable a confirmation of her worst fears. She was left holding onto a device that was now nothing more than an artifact of a life, and a love, that was no more.

Overwhelmed by the suffocating reality, Megumi buried her head into her hands, her shoulders trembling with the weight of her grief. The room, once a haven of shared laughter and cherished memories, now echoed with the sound of her sobs. Uncontrollable, gut-wrenching cries filled every corner, bouncing off the walls and sinking into the carpet. Strangled noises of grief and despair slipped through her fingers, a raw testament to her pain. Her heartache spilled out, cascading in a wave of tears that soaked the sleeves of her shirt. Every inch of her being ached with the absence of the man who was no longer more than a voice on a machine, leaving her in a world that suddenly felt too big, too empty.

With trembling fingers, Megumi quickly typed out a terse email: "Apologies, but I'm feeling unwell and need to cancel our meetings for the day." After a swift glance at her contact list, she selected a few recipients, hit send, and then shut down her computer. Her work for the day was done—her body and soul yearned for the comfort of home and the solace of rest.

Stepping out onto the busy city street, Megumi was enveloped by the familiar cacophony of city noise. She raised a hand to hail a taxi, her heart pounding in rhythm with the city's hustle and bustle. As the black taxi cab pulled up beside her, the driver hopped out and opened the door, his welcoming smile a stark contrast to the gloom that hung over Megumi. She murmured her address and slid into the backseat, the door closing behind her with a resonating thud. As the taxi merged back into the relentless flow of traffic, she leaned back into the seat, her eyes fixed on the world passing by through the crystal clear window. Suddenly alone with her thoughts, she braced herself for the long ride home.

As the cityscape unfurled outside the taxi window, Megumi's gaze fell upon the familiar landmarks, each a poignant echo of the shared past with Ryan. There was the quaint little café where they had savored cups of coffee, their laughter blending with the aromatic scent of freshly ground beans. Across the street stood the park with its ancient, sprawling oak under which they had lounged during one beautiful, sunlit afternoon. Each place was a painful reminder of what was lost, a ghost of a happier time. An involuntary lump formed in her throat as tears welled up in her eyes. She blinked rapidly, a feeble attempt to stem the tide of her grief. It was a futile battle, and she knew it. But for the moment, she clung onto the fragments of her composure, steeling herself against the onslaught of memories.

She had to get home. She had to get home now.

Stepping out of the taxi, Megumi made her way to the entrance of the towering building she called home. The lobby, usually bustling with life, was quiet and deserted at this hour. She rode the elevator up to the penthouse, her heart pounding with each ascending floor. As the doors opened, she found herself standing in the hallway of her luxury penthouse. The once lively and vibrant space suddenly seemed too huge, too empty – a hollow echo of the life she used to share with Ryan.

Megumi fumbled with the keys, finally unlocking the door to her penthouse. She stepped inside, the penthouse's usual welcoming warmth replaced by an unbearable coldness. The luxury couldn't mask the loneliness; it was too quiet, too pristine, too perfect. She felt the emptiness echoing around her, every corner whispering memories of Ryan. It was as if the penthouse was grieving too, mourning the loss of its happy inhabitants.

She walked through the silent corridors, her footsteps resonating in the vast emptiness. She ventured into her bedroom, the room they used to share. The sight of their bed, where they had spent countless nights wrapped in each other's arms, was too much for her. Unable to bear the overwhelming surge of emotions, she fell onto the bed, clutching Ryan's pillow tightly against her chest. And then, the dam broke. Megumi buried her face in the pillow, her body trembling as sobs wracked through her. The penthouse was filled with her cries, a harsh symphony of grief and loss.

Hours had slipped away unnoticeably, and there Megumi was, curled up on the couch. The once full bottle of wine now stood nearly empty on the short table beside her, silently testifying to her desperate attempt to drown her sorrows. Her face, still streaked with the tracks of dried tears, was a canvas of raw emotion. The light in her eyes seemed to have dimmed and her shoulders drooped, weighed down by an unseen burden. The once lively and energetic Megumi was replaced by a shell of her former self, visibly heartbroken and lost in the vast ocean of her own grief. Her penthouse, once a haven of joy and love, now mirrored her state - somber and lifeless.

Megumi was half-asleep when she felt a gentle touch on her shoulder. The touch was so familiar, so comforting, it seemed to resonate with warmth and tenderness. Barely daring to believe, she slowly opened her eyes, blinking the sleep away. Her breath hitched in her throat as she saw a figure standing over her. It was Ryan. He was here, in their penthouse, standing right in front of her. She blinked again, half-expecting him to disappear like a fragment of her countless dreams. But he didn't. Ryan was indeed standing there, an expression of concern and love etched onto his face. For a moment, she lay there, unable to comprehend the reality. The sight of him, alive and standing before her, was so overwhelmingly surreal that she couldn't trust her own senses. She reached out hesitant-ly, her hand shaking as she touched his face, half-expecting her fingers to pass through like a ghost. But they didn't. He was real, and he was here.

Ryan's eyes were flooded with genuine concern as he gazed at Megu-mi. "Are you okay?" he softly inquired. His voice was tender, filled with worry and the hint of a fear he was trying hard to conceal. His question hung in the air, a poignant reminder of their shared past and the intri-cate tapestry of emotions that were woven into their relationship. Con-cerned, he continues, "What's wrong? What happened?"

Megumi stared at Ryan, her eyes wide and questioning. Slowly, she reached a trembling hand to touch his face again, as though to assure herself of his physical presence. She gulped down the lump in her throat, her voice barely above a whisper as she managed to say, *"You're alive?"*. The words hung heavy in the air, filled with disbelief, hope and a silent prayer. It was a question she had longed to ask, the answer to which held the power to mend her broken heart or shatter it irreparably.

Ryan chuckled, he looked at the bottle of wine on the table, "Yeah, I'm alive? Are you okay?"

She sits up, she is still intoxicated. The full bottle of wine, mixed with grief hit her hard. Happiness washes over her face, "Your plane? It crashed? There were no survivors?" He grins, "Are you sure you're okay? My plane didn't crash? I'm here." She jumps up and hugs him tightly. She begins to kiss him passionately. He pulls back to examine her "What happened? My plane didn't crash? I'm here. I'm home."

Megumi is trying to catch her breath, "Your plane, flight 287. It crashed. There were no survivors. I called you so many times and you never answered?"

Ryan starts to process the news. He takes a deep breath, "Holy shit. I wasn't on 287. I got moved to another flight last minute. It crashed?"

She nods, still unable to really speak coherently, "It crashed. Everyone died. I thought I lost you!"

This revelation starts to sink in on Ryan. He is in disbelief. Megumi continues, "I called you. I called so many times but you never picked up?" He nods, "Oh fuck. When I called you from the cab, I must have set my phone down or something. I lost it. That's why I didn't text you about the flight change."

Tears started to flow from Megumi's eyes again. This time they were tears of joy. Happiness washed over her in a way that she thought she would never feel again. The man who made her feel loved, safe and complete was in her arms once again. Again, she pulled in to hug him. He is still in shock over the news. She held him tightly, never wanting to let him go. "I never want to be away from you again. If we travel, we travel together. I can never lose you. I thought I lost you. My life would never.."

He looks at her and nods, "We will always be together. I promise you."

She nods. Still in a state of disbelief and joy. He takes a deep breath, "But I am exhausted. Let's go to bed?" She nods and they make their way to the bedroom.

CHAPTER THIRTY-EIGHT
Unbridled

Ryan and Megumi made their way to the bedroom, the evening's revelations casting a surreal glow over their surroundings. Ryan, glancing at the clock on the wall, noted the late hour. "I need a shower," he announced. Megumi merely nodded in response, her tear-streaked face still etched with relief and disbelief.

As Ryan headed to the bathroom, Megumi moved towards the large oak wardrobe. She quietly undressed, her movements mechanical and absent of their usual grace. Wearing nothing but her lace underwear, she climbed into the large, king-sized bed, the cool sheets providing a welcome contrast against her skin.

In the adjoining room, Ryan let the warm water wash over him, his mind still attempting to process the events of the evening. Meanwhile, in the quiet solitude of their bedroom, Megumi suddenly needed to see him, be in the same room as him, as the events of the day still echoed in her mind. Gracefully, she makes her way out of the bed and into the bathroom.

As the steam swirled around him, Ryan turned off the shower and through the glass he noticed a figure entering the room. It was Megumi. His heart fluttered as he saw her standing there, her silhouette illuminated by the dim bathroom light. He opened the glass door slightly, water droplets cascading down onto the cool tile. His gaze met hers, "Everything okay?" She nods, "I just, I just really wanted to be next to you. See you and make sure I wasn't dreaming. I thought I lost you." He gives her a warm and comforting smile." She walks over to him and they embrace. She slips out of her panties, and removes her bra. She steps into the shower with him. Ryan runs his finger down the side of her face, down on to her neck and along her arm. She trembled with desire as she looks into his piercing blue eyes. They begin to kiss.

Stepping out of the shower, their hair still dripping wet, Ryan and Megumi found their way back to the comfort of the king-sized bed. The soft glow of the bedside lamp cast a warm light across their bodies as they intertwined with each other. Ryan gently pushed back a damp strand of Megumi's hair, his gaze never leaving hers as he traced the contours of her face with his fingertips. Their bodies moved in a synchronic dance, a beautiful display of love and longing. Each touch, each kiss, spoke volumes about their deep-seated love. In the quiet serenity of their room, they found solace in each other's arms, completely consumed by the passionate love they shared.

CHAPTER THIRTY-NINE

Unwelcome Visitors

Today unfolded unlike any other. Around the office there was a heightened sense of relief and joy. The office was buzzing with activity, the clatter of keyboards and the hum of coffee machines providing a familiar soundtrack to their day. Ryan, seated at his office, was engrossed in a new project proposal, his focus unwavering. Just up the posh hallway, Megumi was at her desk, immersed in a design layout. The storm that had been looming over them seemed to have passed, replaced by a serene calmness. Throughout the day, they would find reasons to send each other a text, or pass by the other's office and share a romantic, knowing smile.

Megumi felt an overwhelming sense of optimism. The fear and uncertainty from the past few days were slowly replaced with hope and happiness. She relished the routine, took comfort in the mundanity of her tasks, and found joy in the simplest of things. The occasional shared glance with Ryan, the aroma of freshly brewed coffee, the satisfaction of a task well executed - all felt amplified by her newfound positivity.

Just as the calm of the day was setting in, an unusual disruption occurred. The door to the reception area swung open, revealing the imposing figures of two older men, their faces stern and serious. Their eyes were hard, their suits impeccably tailored, and their aura was one of grave importance. They are obviously Yakuza, a sight that was rare in this office.

As they entered, they were greeted by Kimiko, the office's young receptionist. Kimiko, a woman of unassuming beauty, was taken aback by the sight of the men. Despite the nervous butterflies fluttering in her stomach, she plastered a professional smile on her face, greeted them courteously, and asked them their business. Little did anyone in the office suspect of the imminent upheaval these visitors were about to invoke. Stone faced, one of the Yakuza spoke, "We are here for Megumi Sato." Kimiko tried to force a courteous smile, "Do you have an appointment? I will let her know you are here." The older Yakuza stared at Kimiko a long moment before handing her a business card without saying a word. His eyes seemed to study Kimiko for a reaction. The second Yakuza, sensing Kimiko's sudden apprehension, flashed an ominous smile. Kimiko took a deep breath to steady herself.

Meanwhile, Ryan was standing in Megumi's office. They were in the midst of a light-hearted conversation, discussing their dinner plans for the evening. Ryan, with his casual demeanor, was leaning against the edge of Megumi's desk, while she sat comfortably in her chair, the cityscape creating a beautiful backdrop behind her through the office's large windows. "How about that new Italian place around the corner?" Ryan suggested, his eyes lighting up at the thought of the pasta and wine they might share. Megumi laughed, toying with the pendant of her necklace, and responded, "No breadsticks though. Otherwise, I will never fit into my wedding dress!" Ryan chuckles, "You're a size zero. You have no worries. Trust me. You will be the most beautiful bride in history." She grins, "You spoil me Ryan." He chuckles, "Better get used to it. I'm only getting started."

Megumi's playful smile fades like falling snow on warm concrete.

Her expression turns serious, "I need to step out for a moment. I will be right back." Ryan notices her shift, "Everything okay? What's up?" She fakes a smile, "Yes. Everything is fine. I will be right back." She stands up to leave, Ryan can tell something is off, there is a stiffness to her words. "Want me to wait here?" She smiles, a warm and sincere smile breaks through the look of apprehension only a moment ago. She loves him so much, and he makes her feel safe and supported in a way that she has never felt before. "I will be right back." She makes her way from the office and Ryan watches her leave, his concern from a moment ago washed away by her smile.

Megumi makes her way to the elevator, her heart pounding in her chest. As the doors open, she steps into the lobby of the building. Kimiko and Megumi share a quick and awkward glance. Kimiko puts her head down and pretends to work. Megumi stiffens as she approaches the two men.

Megumi looks at the two Yakuza. Her words are confident, but inside she is trembling, "Let's not talk here." She looks around the lobby nervously. Being seen talking with Yakuza in the lobby of the company where she is the CEO... that would not be good. The older of the two Yakuza gives her an expressionless nod. The younger one grins. They make their way out of the lobby and out of sight.

Moments later, Megumi enters the lobby. She is shaken, but trying to hide it. As she makes her way to the elevator she is met by Ryan. Instantly Ryan knows something is off, "You okay? What happened?" She nods, "I'm fine." The tone of her voice, and the look in her eyes, Ryan can tell that's not true. Instinctively he looks up. He knows the truth is outside. He makes his way to the door and out of sight.

Just outside of the building, the two Yakuza are walking away. Not really walking, more like swaggering. They are laughing and looking around as though they own the city. In a sort of way, they do. This part of Tokyo at least. As they walk, they are oblivious to Ryan approaching from behind. Ryan walks quickly to catch up. About twenty feet behind them, Ryan calls with an anger they are not used to hearing, not from a civilian at least, "Hey." Instinctively they stop and turn. The older Yakuza has a stone faced glare to him. The younger one flashes a slimy grin. Ryan looks them up and down, "Were you just in my building?" The younger Yakuza laughs, "Your building? Nothing here is yours you fucking foreigner. Go back to England." The older Yakuza nods, "I was."

Ryan walks up closer. He is now just five feet away. His look is intense as he stares at the older Yakuza. He glances over at the younger one for a moment and back to the older one, who is obviously the leader of the two, "Were you talking to Megumi?" The older one nods, "I was. What is it to you?" The older Yakuza stares at Ryan. The younger one chimes in, "Yeah, what is it to you?" Ryan gives the younger one a look before adding, "You shut the fuck up. You're totally irrelevant here. And I am not English, I am American. Fucking piece of shit." The younger Yakuza is shocked. His blood is boiling, but he knows he cannot take action without the approval of the older one, who truly is his leader. The older Yakuza looks at Ryan with a bewildered look of respect. Sometimes people talk back, but never with an intensity that actually concerns them. Something about Ryan is different. The older Yakuza takes a deep breath, "We have business with Miss Sato."

Ryan shakes his head as he steps closer, "Not anymore. You understand me?" The older Yakuza just looks at Ryan. The younger Yakuza makes a noise, almost like a grunt, but more guttural. Ryan looks over to him as the younger Yakuza opens up his coat to show that he has a knife in his waistband. He flashes an arrogant look. Ryan wheels and punches the younger Yakuza hard in the stomach, knocking him to the ground. Instantly he delivers a kick, a very hard kick to the young man's face, blood instantly pooling on the unbelievably clean white concrete. The older Yakuza grabs Ryan and looks into his eyes, "Control yourself. Stop now."

Ryan breathes heavy as he looks into the older Yakuza's eyes. They share a strange look of mutual respect. Ryan nods that he will stop. The older Yakuza looks at his colleague, still laying on the ground writhing in pain. He looks back to Ryan, "Go back in your building, now." Ryan nods at the older Yakuza, and back at the younger one, still on the ground, before walking back to the office.

Ryan enters the lobby. Instantly Megumi walks up to Ryan quickly. Her voice trembling. It's clear that she saw the scene unfold outside, "Are you okay?" Ryan, still breathing heavily from the adrenaline dump only a few minutes ago. He nods, "I am going to fucking kill those guys." Megumi pulls back and shakes her head, "No. I am going to find them and apologize. I need to fix this."

Ryan is shocked, "Fix this? What business did they have with you anyhow? Fix this?" Megumi shakes her head, "You don't understand. They control this part of the city. They are very powerful. And dangerous." Ryan repeats himself, "What business did they have with you?" Megumi takes a deep breath, "Meet me at home. I will explain."

Ryan just looks at her. She continues, "Go back home now.. please? I will get your things and meet you there. I will come along shortly." Ryan nods solemnly before walking away. Megumi watches Ryan exit the building before she hurries over to the elevator. Her mind racing with the revelation she needs to share with Ryan. The head start she gave him will be very valuable in figuring out how she will tell him.

CHAPTER FORTY

Shadowverse Explained

Back in her luxury penthouse, Ryan and Megumi sat on her plush white couch, facing each other. The panoramic glass wall revealed the city's neon glow, providing an eerie backdrop to their serious conversation. Megumi's face was a study in solemnity, a stark contrast to the usually jovial expression she wore.

"I owed the Yakuza a favor," she began, her voice barely above a whisper. Ryan's eyebrows shot up in surprise, but he remained silent, urging her to continue. "They... they own me in a way. They want me to go back to dancing at Shadowverse."

Megumi paused, gauging Ryan's reaction. He sat still, his face a mask, processing the information. She took a deep breath and continued, "I didn't have a choice, Ryan. They protected me when I had nobody, and nothing."

She glanced nervously at Ryan, awaiting his reaction. Outside, the city's lights glittered, oblivious of the bombshell that had just been dropped in the penthouse above.

Ryan was trying to process this. Deep down, he knew this was the case. He wasn't sure if his violent reaction outside of the building was driven by a need to protect her, or his jealousy at the thought of other men watching her dance, dirty thoughts in their minds.

He nods, "I thought you danced there because you wanted to? You are their property?" He watched her for a reaction. Tears welled up in her eyes, "I am not their property, but I was one of their more.. popular dancers." Now it is her, studying him for a reaction. He just nodded, "I love you Megumi. With all of my heart. If you told me that you wanted to go back to dancing there, I would be okay with it. But only if you wanted to. I am not going to lie, I would feel jealous. It wouldn't be fun for me, but I would respect it. And I would support you."

She starts to speak but he cuts her off and continues, "But I am not going to let them force you into it. I will kill them. I will kill every fucking one of them. Even if I died in the process."

With a slight nod, she caresses Ryan's face, "I can fix this Ryan. I have a way. I just need to talk with the right people. I am not going to dance there... ever again. We are together, and you are the only man I want to see me like that. For the rest our lives. Please trust me?"

Ryan does trust her. He trusts her in a way he never thought possible. The drama and upset of the day has suddenly disappeared. He feels good again. She feels it and he feels it. Ryan's cell phone buzzes in his pocket. He tries to ignore it. As soon as it stops, it starts again. Questions run through his mind, he almost never gets calls. Maybe it was the office asking where he is and why he disappeared so abruptly?

Just then Megumi smiled, "Would you like a drink?" He nods. She gets up and makes her way to the kitchen. Ryan pulls his phone out of his pocket. He has an array of missed calls and texts from Kazu. Instantly Ryan knew what this was about.

Megumi returns to the sofa with two gin and tonics in hand. Even with Ryan's mind going over the various scenarios in his head why Kazu would be reaching out, he marvels at her elegance at how she moves. She doesn't just move, she glides. She hands Ryan his drink and she holds hers up and they toast, "Kampai" she adds. He takes a sip before excusing himself to the restroom.

Inside the restroom he quickly shuts the door and pulls his phone from his pocket. He texts Kazu and he waits.

Chapter Forty-One

Family Ties

Ryan exits the restroom, his mind a whirlwind of thoughts and apprehensions. He takes one last long look at Megumi, who's engrossed in an old movie playing on the television. He assures her he'll be back soon, citing a sudden errand he needs to run. She understands, always understanding, and waves him goodbye with a knowing smile.

Stepping outside, Ryan hails a cab. As he makes his way through the labyrinth of Tokyo's streets, he watches the city lights dancing across the skyline. The city is alive with a rhythm all of its own, a pulse that Ryan now finds himself a part of. He can't help but marvel at the way life has brought him to this vibrant metropolis, to Megumi, and now, back to the Shadowverse club.

The cab pulls up outside the Shadowverse club and Ryan pays the driver before stepping out. The familiarity of the club's exterior brings a wave of nostalgia and a hint of anxiety for what the next hour has in store. Kazu called him here, and he needed to come. What would unfold could be anybody's guess.

Ryan makes his way into the club. Even under these dangerous circumstances, he marvels at the sheer elegance of the club, and the dancers. Tonight though, the dancers looked bizarre to him. He could not really even look at them without feeling a sense of guilt - guilt to the woman he loves, sitting at home trusting him, and at the guilt that each of these women held a secret, and a story that propelled them to be on display like this. As this ran through his mind, Kazu approached, "Oi." Kazu motioned to him.

Kazu and Ryan make their way down a hallway, neither saying a word. They enter through a door marked "Private" in Japanese, and in English. As they enter, Ryan immediately recognizes the older Yakuza from the confrontation outside of his building. He is sitting at a low slung table, a glass of whiskey in front of him alongside a pack of Marlboro Red cigarettes.

Instantly, thoughts ran through his mind that Kazu set him up. He shoots Kazu a look of shock an fear. Kazu nods, "It's okay my friend. It's okay." The older Yakuza finally smiles. Not really a smile, but a smirk - almost that Ryan's fearful glance was the validation he needed. He motioned Ryan to sit down. Ryan takes a deep breath and sits down.

Ryan starts to speak and the man's smirk disappeared, his stone faced glare replacing it, "We have a mutual friend it appears." The older Yakuza grunts out. Ryan looks to Kazu and Kazu nods, he is visibly pleased. The older Yakuza continues, "You're not afraid of Yakuza?"

Ryan reads the room perfectly, "I am very afraid of Yakuza. And I have a lot of respect for Yakuza. I know full well the violence you are capable of." The man bows his head slightly at the perceived complement before inquiring, "But it sounds like Kazu-san tried to hustle you, and you didn't cower. Is that true? Are you not afraid of Kazu-san? He is very intimidating."

Ryan nods his head, "He did, and yes, I did not cower. And yes, he is very intimidating." Ryan looks over to Kazu, and Kazu bows his head slightly. The older Yakuza continues, "If you were intimidated, why didn't you cower?"

As Ryan thought over his next sentence, the older Yakuza took a drink from his whiskey before pulling one of the cigarettes out of the pack. As he reaches for his lighter, Ryan interrupts and picks it up. He flicks the lighter and it produces a flame that he touches to the older Yakuza's cigarette. The older Yakuza nods in appreciation before taking the pack and offering one to Ryan and Kazu. Both accept and Ryan lights Kazu's before lighting his own. They each take a drag and Ryan continues, "I didn't cower because there are some things in life that are worse than death." The older Yakuza nods. Kazu smiles. Kazu adds, "You thought I was going to kill you?" with a chuckle. Ryan was not laughing, "Kazu-san, you are a scary guy. I thought it was a possibility."

The older Yakuza is curious, "You said that some things are worse than death?" Ryan nods. The older man continues, "What could be worse than death?"

Before Ryan can answer, a beautiful hostess with a short skirt and bikini top enters with a tray of drinks. The men watch silently as she sets the drinks down and leaves. Kazu stares lustfully at her as she leaves.

Ryan resumes, "What could be worse than death?" He pauses before going on, "Cowering in the face of somebody trying to bully me. That is worse than death." The older Yakuza loves this. He smiles in a way that others rarely see out of him. He picks up his glass and raises a toast, "Kampai."

The three mean toast. Only hours ago, Ryan was toasting with Megumi. Life has a funny way of changing on a dime. They each take a drink from their glasses. The older Yakuza sets his glass down. His smile quickly fades back into the ominous stare from before.

The older Yakuza stares with a hostile look that takes Ryan by surprise. The man glares at Ryan before speaking, "We have a very serious problem that you caused earlier today. You hurt one of my men.. badly.

I cannot let that go." Ryan nods, his fearful feelings returning. The older Yakuza continues, "What are you willing to do to make up for it?"

Ryan looks to Kazu who is now looking serious. Very serious. The older Yakuza looks back at Ryan, his voice calm and quiet, but with a deadly undertone, "What are you willing to do to make up for it?"

Ryan takes a deep breath, going back to the strategy that has worked for him so far, "Like I said before. I have a lot of respect for you. And your organization. I know you are a very powerful man. I don't feel that I was in the wrong, but if you say I was.. then I was. I am ready to accept any punishment you feel is appropriate."

The older Yakuza reaches under the low slung sofa and pulls out a short sword, wrapped in a white cloth. Ryan knew what this meant. The older Yakuza wants Ryan to cut off the tip of his pinky finger. Suddenly his pulse quickens. The older Yakuza sees the look of concern in Ryan's eyes before asking, "In the Yakuza, when a soldier makes a mistake, he cuts off the tip of one of his little fingers. It is a form of apology. It shows sincerity. Have you heard of this before?" Ryan nods yes. A mix of queasiness and fear setting in. The older Yakuza continues, "Do you why this tradition exists?"

Ryan's mind starts to race. How will he explain this to Megumi? He said he was running and errand, and now, he is going to come home with a missing finger? How will he work? How will he type? What will he tell his family back in the U.S.? The icy glare of the older Yakuza brings him back to reality. He needs to answer, and he needs to answer now. His finger, or even his life, may be hanging in the balance of the next few minutes.

Ryan shakes his head, "No, I don't." The older Yakuza continues, "In the early days of the Yakuza, hundreds of years ago, our disputes were settled with swords. When a man loses a finger, it reduces the grip he has on a sword. This makes the man fully dependent on his Oyabun for his very survival."

Ryan nods. The older Yakuza just nods for a moment. He puts the short sword on the table next to their drinks. "How the hell did this turn so bad, so fast?" Ryan thinks to himself. The older Yakuza studying Ryan for emotion, "Are you willing to cut your finger to atone for your mistake?"

Ryan looks the man dead in the eye and nods his head, "Yes. I am. If this is what it takes for you to respect me. I will do it."

The older Yakuza nods, "There is one other matter to discuss. Megumi Sato returning to dance here at the club. I run this club, and her absence is costing me money."

Ryan, at hearing Megumi's name mentioned by this man, and how he is the one trying to pull her back into the club.. makes him want to remove the sword and stick it through his heart. As Ryan fights to suppress his emotions, the older Yakuza makes an offer, "Would you be willing to lose a second finger? To release her from that obligation?"

Ryan is shocked at the question, but even more shocked at his own quick reply, "Yes. I will do it. Right now." Ryan removes the short sword from its scabbard and puts his hand on the table. The older Yakuza abruptly blurts out, "No. Not like that. There is a proper way to do this." It totally breaks the silence and shatters the mood. Ryan looks up startled. The man reaches over and takes the sword from Ryan. He slides the sword back under the sofa.

Ryan sits dumbfounded. The older Yakuza takes a drink as Ryan just watches. The older Yakuza pulls out another cigarette, and again Ryan lights it. As the man takes a deep drag he tells Ryan "What you saw at your office today was not be forcing Megumi Sato back to this club. I was asking her to fulfill a promise she made to me years ago. A promise that she dutifully kept until you came in to her life. She told me that she is in love with you, and she did not want to return. She wants to marry you and completely change her life." Ryan smiles, as he thinks to himself, "She said that?" His happiness quickly fades as he remembers the situation unfolding in front of him.

The older Yakuza looks to Kazu. Kazu interjects, "Meg is my sister. She was never in danger."

Ryan is shocked. The older Yakuza looks at Ryan, "As you can see. She was never in danger. Kazu-san has been a loyal soldier since he was just a teen. I would never hurt him... or his sister."

Ryan is still in shock, "Megumi... is your sister?" Kazu nods stoically.

The older Yakuza looks at Ryan. A mix of fatherly love and pride in his eyes, "I have known her since they both were children. I got her to the top of her company. She does owe me, but she owes me her loyalty, not her body. I would never hurt her."

Ryan struggles to get his words out, "I had.. no idea." The older Yakuza is not even listening to Ryan as he interrupts, "And my associate that you hurt. I need you to fix that. Understood?" Ryan nods, "Anything you want. I will do it."

The older Yakuza nods, "You need to pay for his medical bills. When he recovers, take him for drinks. Kazu will tell you the nightclub. Can you do that?" Ryan is curious, "Take him for drinks?" The older Yakuza persists, a deadly serious tone, "Take him for drinks. Yes. Can you do that?" Ryan nods, "No problem at all. Consider this done."

Kazu stands and nods to Ryan. Ryan also stands. As the two turn to leave, the older Yakuza calls to them, "One other thing. If I ever need a favor, then you will be there for me?" Ryan nods, "No problem. Yes. Anything you need... and thank you. Thank you for getting past that thing that happened, and thank you for letting Megumi retire from dancing.

I truly appreciate it."

The older Yakuza nods. "You have my word. And I have yours? If I need a favor, you will repay it, no questions asked?" Ryan nods energetically, "Yes, you have my word. Anything you need."

As Ryan and Kazu leave the room, Ryan feels like the weight of the world has just been lifted from him.

As soon as Ryan and Kazu step out into the hallway, Ryan looks to Kazu, "Megumi is your sister?" Kazu nods. Ryan is left standing in the hallway as Kazu walks away without even looking back.

CHAPTER FORTY-TWO

Home Sweet Home

Ryan returns home, the tension of the day dissolving as he steps into the familiar warmth of his house. His eyes follow a trail of rose petals leading from the front door, their soft fragrance filling the air. It's a path designed with love and care, a path that leads him to their large, elegant bathroom. The petals end at the foot of a bathtub, casting a romantic glow in the dimly lit room.

In the bathtub, Megumi waits for him, her face lit up with a soft smile. The water gently laps around her, steam rising in the air and creating an ethereal atmosphere. The day's events seem like a distant memory in this moment, as if they've been locked outside the confines of their home. The tension in Ryan's body seeps away, replaced by a warmth that has nothing to do with the temperature of the room. In this moment, he is home, truly home. His gaze locks with Megumi's, a silent conversation passing between them. This is their sanctuary, a place where the world and its problems have no place.

Megumi offers a tender smile, "How were your errands?" Ryan just looks at her. He has no idea how he will tell her about his meeting. She flashes a seductive smile, "I was hoping you would join me." He nods as he starts to undress, "I met your brother tonight." Her look of seductive elegance is quickly replaced by surprise.

Some time has passed and Ryan and Megumi are in the bath, her head laying back on Ryan's shoulder, listening to him as he told the story of how the night unfolded. She turns to look at Ryan, her expression serious. "You need to understand. He is a serious man. They are serious people. It is not good to owe him a favor. He *will* ask you to repay it. You don't know how serious this is." Ryan nods. "You're free from the club now. That's good, right?." She smiles sweetly. "You're the sweetest and bravest man in the world... and you are all mine. What can I ever do to repay you?" Her seductive smile returns. He grins. She starts to kiss him passionately, "Take me to bed?" He grins, "Let's go."

As they make their way to their bedroom, the dazzling lights of Tokyo create a vibrant tapestry outside their windows. Their bodies silhouette against the glowing cityscape, dancing to the rhythm of their hearts. Their clothes are discarded, the serious conversations of the evening forgotten in the face of their shared desire. Ryan's hands explore the contours of Megumi's body, each touch eliciting a sound of pleasure that spills into the night. Their bodies move in a synchronized dance, the city lights flickering mimicking their passion. Shadows dance across their skin as the city sleeps beneath them, oblivious to the symphony playing out above. Their love making is a mix of passionate desperation and tender exploration - a silent testament to their bond. Their silhouettes merge and part, caught in a dance as old as time itself, under the twinkling Tokyo sky. Their shared breaths and whispered words fill the room, the city's soundscape providing a distant hum in the background. As they find their completion, they fall into each other's arms, the city lights casting an ethereal glow over their entwined forms. The world outside continues to spin, unaware of the profound love declared in their bedroom high above the sprawling metropolis below.

As they lay intertwined, Ryan's curiosity gets the better of him, and he finds himself asking about the older Yakuza he met with earlier in the night. Megumi stiffens slightly in his arms, her reluctance palpable even in the dim light. "He's...he's a serious man," she begins, her voice barely audible above the hum of the city. "He has done many things... hurt many people...killed..." She trails off, the words hanging in the air between them. She buries her face in his chest, unwilling to speak more about the dark figure from her past. The room falls into silence, save for the distant sounds of Tokyo below, the mention of the Yakuza casting a shadow over their post-intimate serenity.

After a long silence, Ryan breaks the quiet with a question that has been nagging at him. "Didn't he save you though?" he asks, his voice echoing slightly in the still room. Megumi lifts her head from his chest and nods, a complicated mix of emotions crossing her features. "Yes...," she admits, her voice barely more than a whisper. "But it's complicated. I owe him a great debt, but he... he still scares me." Her words hang heavily in the air, a testament to the complex web of fear, obligation, and gratitude that binds her to the shadowy figure from her past. Ryan decides not to press her on this. His mind drifting towards the future implications of the promise he made. As he drifts off to sleep, his thoughts are haunted by the Yakuza and his now solid ties to them.

CHAPTER FORTY-THREE

One Month Later

A month had passed since that fateful night when the Yakuza's shadow cast a pall over their tranquility. The metropolis of Tokyo, with its neon lights and ceaseless energy, continued to pulse beneath them, indifferent to their own personal dramas. Life had been surprisingly calm, offering them a respite to heal, grow, and find comfort in each other.

Ryan and Megumi were both thriving at work. Although their colleagues knew that they were romantically involved, nobody seemed to mind. Quite the opposite in fact. Ryan worked hard and was a great team player - and ever since Ryan came in to her life, she seemed more balanced, more upbeat and openly encouraged people to have a healthier work / life balance.

Despite the hum of activity around them, an unexpected lull in Megumi's afternoon arrived when Ryan popped his head into her office. His hair was slightly disheveled from the day's work and his eyes twinkled with an unspoken proposal. "Fancy hitting golf balls at the driving range later this evening?" he asked, with a casual, almost nonchalant air. Megumi looked up from her desk, her surprise quickly giving way to a bright smile. "Are you asking me on a date?," she grinned, He chuckled, "Nothing serious, but yeah, I guess you can call it a date." Playfully, she shoots back, "Okay, as long as it's nothing serious.. I guess we can hit the driving range. Seven o'clock?" He nods.

CHAPTER FORTY-FOUR

Hitting that Perfect Shot

Under the soft glow of the setting summer sun, the driving range was a patchwork of emerald and gold. Ryan and Megumi, in their casual golf attire, added a dash of color to the scene. Their laughter echoed through the evening air as they took turns driving golf balls down the range.

Ryan, in his polo shirt and beige slacks, was the embodiment of casual elegance. His natural athleticism was reflected in his every move, from his confident stride to the way he effortlessly swung the club. Megumi, on the other hand, looked chic in her tailored golf shorts and a vibrant top, her hair gathered in a neat ponytail. With each swing, she displayed a grace that was uniquely hers, a testament to her unyielding spirit.

Their shared enjoyment of the evening was evident in their relaxed demeanors and easy smiles. The pressures of their recent friction with the Yakuza and their demanding jobs seemed to fade into the background, at least for a little while. There in the glow of the setting sun, life was simple. It was just two people, their shared laughter, the crisp sound of golf clubs hitting balls, and the promise of many more such moments to come.

Ryan steadies himself, swings his club and comes up short, hitting the green artificial turf with an awkward thud. Megumi looks over and grins. Confidently he raises his eyebrows, as another ball pops up on the automated tee. Again, he takes another swing, and this time the result is even worse. Megumi chuckles, "You okay over there?" He smiles. Another ball pops up on the tee and again, he absolutely shanks it. Megumi looks over to him, "Watch this." She swings, the picture of focused elegance. Her club glides through the air and connection between club and ball is perfect. The ball leaves the club and slices through the air, straight as an arrow and off into the heavy night air. She looks over and grins. "How was that?" She asks rhetorically. Ryan cocks his head to the side, "Looked like a lucky shot to me." She just smiles. Ryan motions to his bag, "Can you grab me my gloves? My hands are sweaty." She grins, she is not used to Ryan ever asking her to do anything for him. Quite the opposite actually. In all of the time that they have been together, he has been the picture of the doting boyfriend. Slightly impatiently, he asks again, "Can you please.. grab me my gloves?" This time he had a hint of annoyance in his voice. She was not used to this. Now she is slightly annoyed. She gives him a long look before going over to his bag, and looking over, "Where are they?" He just nods, "Bottom compartment." Slightly annoyed, she takes a deep breath, unzips the bottom compartment of his high end golf bag and she reaches in. "No gloves in here." He points, "Down in the bottom." She reaches deeper, and pulls out a small box. He walks over, "Here, give that to me. The gloves have to be in there." His voice even more annoyed than before. He walks over to her, takes the box from her hand and she reaches back into the bag. She looks back to him. "Not in here."

Ryan nods his head, "Damn. Okay. I guess they are not in there." He opens up the box and feigns a look of surprise, "Oh damn. Look at this." He turns the box to show Megumi the contents of the small, and now open, box. It's a beautiful diamond engagement ring. Megumi's look of exasperation turns to one of shock.. and joy. A huge smile washes over her face. "Is that..?" Ryan nods before getting down on one knee before her. He looks up at her, his eyes filled with love and sincerity. "Megumi, I have loved you since the moment I met you. I knew, in that very moment, that I would love you for the rest of my life. When you are away from me, even for a moment, I feel like a piece of me is missing. Would you please make me complete and be my wife?"

Still shocked, she nods yes before hugging him tightly. They begin to kiss passionately. "Is that a yes?" He asks with a silly grin on his face. "Yes. That is a yes. One hundred percent yes."

He pulls back slightly, "I can't start our marriage with a lie. I didn't really need the gloves." He grins. She just nods and smiles as he continues, "And I didn't really shank those shots. That was also a lie." She nods, feigning exasperation, "And what's all of this stuff about tonight being nothing serious? That was a lie?" He grins, "You caught me. That was also a lie."

They look deeply into each others eyes. Their looks communicating a depth of love that many seek but very few ever find. Megumi finally breaks the silence, "I tried so hard to push you away. I was so scared that if you knew who I was, who I really was, you would walk away. And that terrified me." Ryan kisses her tenderly and pulls back, again, looking deeply in to her eyes. "I will never leave you. I will always take care of you to the absolute best of my ability. I love you, all of you, more than you can ever know." Tears begin to well up in her eyes, "I do know. I really do. You are all I want. Forever."

Time stands still as they peer into each others eyes, oblivious to the throbbing pulse of the city in the distance.

As the night matured, Ryan and Megumi found themselves nestled in a corner booth of an elegant restaurant, surrounded by soft candlelight and the delicate clink of glassware. Their conversation flowed effortlessly from laughter-filled reminiscing to exciting future plans for their upcoming wedding.

"I've always thought a beach wedding would be beautiful," Megumi suggested, her eyes sparkling with the reflection of candlelight.

Ryan nodded in agreement, "I can just picture you walking down the aisle with the sunset casting a golden glow on you. It would be perfect."

Their conversation took a playful turn as they moved on to discuss potential honeymoon destinations. "How about honeymooning in Hawaii?" Ryan inquired, raising an eyebrow in anticipation of her reaction.

Megumi rolled her eyes, giggling, "And have you wrestle with a shark to impress me? I don't think so." Their laughter filled the air, creating a symphony of joy that was perfectly tuned to their love story. The night was a promise of their future together - filled with laughter, mutual respect, and deep love.

Just as the laughter started to subside, the restaurant door opened. A distinguished figure stepped in, his transient glance sweeping across the room. It was Kazu, Megumi's brother. Unknown to Megumi, Ryan had planned this surprise reunion. He had reached out to Kazu earlier and invited him to join them. Seeing Kazu, Ryan's eyes sparkled with anticipation, and he subtly nudged Megumi, directing her attention toward the entrance.

Her eyes widened in disbelief, a gasp escaping her lips. "Kazu?", she exclaimed, with a wide eyed look. She looks to Ryan, who gives her a nod and a grin. Kazu walks over to the table. Kazu nods at Ryan, "I hear congratulations are in order?"

Ryan's joy at Kazu's arrival was shadowed by a sudden change in Megumi's demeanor. Her light-heartedness had evaporated, replaced by a chilling silence. Her once sparkling eyes now looked away, avoiding her brother's gaze. Ryan, taken aback by Megumi's reaction, attempted to break the tension. "Kazu, we're delighted you could join us tonight," he said, his voice steady despite the unease gnawing at him. He cast a worried look at Megumi, his mind racing to understand her discomfort. Megumi gives Kazu a forced smile, "Kazu-san, it's very good to see you. It has been a long time." Kazu bows his head slightly, "It is very good to see you too Megu-chan."

The restaurant seemed to echo with an awkward silence, the earlier joviality replaced with palpable tension. The clinking cutlery and murmuring of the other guests seemed to recede into the background, all eyes drawn to the trio at the corner table. Ryan cleared his throat, "Kazu-san," he began tentatively. "Megumi and I would be honored if you could attend our wedding." He paused for a moment, looking at Kazu earnestly. "We both want you there. It would mean a lot to us."

Kazu looked from Ryan to his sister, his face unreadable. The silence stretched on, the earlier tension now replaced with anticipation. After what felt like an eternity, Kazu finally nodded, "I would be honored, Ryan-san." His voice held a note of warmth, his face softening into a small, sincere smile.

Ryan smiles at Kazu, grateful that Megumi's brother has accepted their invitation. It's important to Ryan that he brings their family closer together. Ryan then looks over to Megumi, who looks visibly tense. She is looking down at the elegant meal sitting before her. She looks up from her meal and gives Kazu a forced smile. "Would you like to join us for dinner?" Kazu reads the mood and decides to leave. "I wish I could. I need to go over to Shibuya. There is a new club opening up and I need to introduce myself. But thank you very much for the offer.." Kazu stands up and looks from Megumi to Ryan. "Again, congratulations on your engagement. I look forward to attending." Ryan and Megumi both nod at Kazu before he walks away.

As soon as Kazu disappears from sight, Megumi looks to Ryan with a slightly concerned look. "I know what you are doing, and I appreciate it, but I don't think it's a good idea." Ryan sighs deeply, "He's your brother. He needs to be there. You don't want him there?" Ryan watches Megumi, looking for a response. Again, he asks, "You don't want your brother to attend our wedding?" Nervously, Megumi scans the restaurant, "He is my brother, and I love him, but having a Yakuza at our wedding.. it's not a good idea. It's not safe."

Chapter Forty-Five

Bliss

Months passed and life unfolded like a dream for Ryan and Megumi. With their daily work going remarkably well, they found themselves more in sync than ever before. Ryan was thriving in his role, finding innovative marketing and product solutions for the company, while Megumi really found a new level of performance as CEO. Her charisma and vision took on a whole new dimension and her strategic vision and alliances were resulting in home run after home run. The board was happy, the investors were getting great returns and employee morale was thriving was never higher.

The wedding preparations were also progressing smoothly under Megumi's meticulous planning, and Ryan's thoughtful insights. They found joy in every little detail - from choosing the floral arrangements to sampling the wedding cake flavors. The anticipation of their impending wedding day was more exhilarating than nerve-wracking, and their future together was a beacon of hope and comfort.

Their relationship was never stronger, or more fulfilling. The laughter, shared moments of happiness, and the warm reassurances of love were the new standard in these times. Ryan and Megumi, in their bubble of bliss, savored every moment, looking forward to their wedding day and the promise of a beautiful life together.

Months were passing like minutes in these blissful times. However, there was a storm massing on the horizon, unseen and undetected by the happy couple. It was almost as if the universe was planning a cruel and unthinkable practical joke on them that threatens to rip it all away from them.

Ryan and Megumi were sharing a casual dinner at home when Megumi's cell phone started to buzz. She picked it up and looked at the screen. Ryan noticed her smile and asks, "What's up?" Megumi just smiled as she typed a reply. After hitting send, she looks up, "Kazu, we are having lunch tomorrow." Ryan raises his eyebrows, "Really?" She nods, "I thought about what you said, and you were right. We are having lunch tomorrow. It's time to mend fences like you said." Ryan is curious, "Wow, what prompted that?" Megumi just smiles, it feels like she is hiding a secret, "Nothing really, just thought about what you said, and you were right." Ryan has to dig deeper, "You've been back in touch with him?" She nods with a grin, "Counter to what you may think, I really do listen to you." They both chuckle.

A few minutes have passed and the conversation has been light, drifting from topic to topic. Suddenly, Megumi looks serious, "You really changed me Ryan." Ryan notices the shift, "Changed you?" Megumi nods solemnly, "For as long as I can remember, I lived my life in a shell. I was always afraid to let myself be happy. It was better to never have it, than to have it and lose it. I have lost a lot."

Ryan reaches across the table and takes her hand. She is looking down now. It's clear this is a deeply personal thing for her, "I hated Kazu. I truly hated him. He is the kind of person that no matter what happens to him, he just keeps smiling. He always found a way to be happy and trust that it would last. I wasn't happy at all. I guess you could say that I was envious of him."

Ryan chuckles, "He wasn't too happy when he was trying to shake me down, my first night here in Tokyo." Megumi doesn't even react as she continues, "His work is his work. He has to be mean sometimes to survive, he is just like my father in that way. But he's actually a really kind person. People used to tell me stories about his kindness, how he helped people who had nothing, how he helped kids being bullied. He's done a lot of nice things."

She looks intently into Ryan's eyes, "It's time I believe in happiness. In love." Ryan silently mouths the words, "I love you." She smiles and nods, "I can't lose you Ryan. I simply couldn't go on." Ryan nods at her, "I love you. Forever."

They share a loving smile. Ryan asks, "It's been a long day. Why don't you go get into bed and I will clean this up." She nods, gets up and leaves the room as Ryan starts to clean up the table and take the dishes into the kitchen.

Ryan makes his way into the bedroom to find Megumi already tucked into bed. When she hears Ryan, she sits up and holds out her hand, "I already missed you." He walks over, takes her hand, "I missed you more.. let me go brush my teeth. I'll be right back." He walks from the room and Megumi settles back into the bed before calling out, "Am I crazy for believing in love?"

Ryan reappears, still brushing his teeth. He shakes his head no.

Moments later, Ryan makes his way over to the bed and slides under the covers next to Megumi. He holds her tightly, "As long as it's me that you love, you are not crazy." She laughs and playfully slaps at him, "Of course it's you! Who else would it be?" He grins, "Good answer."

They begin to kiss passionately. The lights of Tokyo shimmering through the floor to ceiling windows.

CHAPTER FORTY-SIX

Mending Fences

On a bright Friday afternoon, the hum of the office chatter was punctuated with the buzz of weekend plans. Ryan sat in his office, engrossed in his work, the steady click-clack of the keyboard echoing in the room. The door creaked open and Megumi walked in, a small stack of papers in her hand and a question in her eyes.

"Ryan," she began, hesitating at the doorframe, "I'm having dinner with Kazu later tonight, is that still okay?" Ryan looked up from his screen, he takes a deep breath, relaxing back in his chair. "Of course. I think that's great. Where are you two going?"

"Ramen, some place over in Kanda." She replies as she walks over and takes a seat in one of the well appointed leather chairs in front of his desk. She smiles cautiously, "I just feel a bit bad. Friday night is always our night. Will you be okay on your own?"

Ryan grins, "I'll be fine. I'll probably go over to the academy and do some Jiu-Jitsu and then over to the spa for a soak and a swim."

Megumi leaned forward, her eyes meeting Ryan's. A tender smile crept up on her lips, one that held an ocean of love and appreciation for the man in front of her. "You're really amazing, you know that?" she said, her voice a soft whisper, laden with emotions. His understanding and support had always been unwavering, and it was in moments like these that she was reminded of just how truly lucky she was to have him.

Ryan responds with a smile of his own. "I'm really happy that you two are having dinner. He's your brother, and mending those fences that have been broken for way too long." Then he chuckles, half jokingly, "Just DO NOT agree to start dancing at his club again. That's all I ask.." Megumi crinkles up her little nose at the thought of it. She playfully lifts up her hand like she would slap him if he were sitting closer. "I would never. I promise you that you are the only man that will ever see me undressed.. ever again." With that, they both smile and chuckle. She stands up to leave. As she goes, she stops and turns back, "I'm going to take off a bit early. I am meeting him at six. But I will come say goodbye first." Ryan just nods with a supportive smile. She leaves the room and Ryan watches her go with a look of love and contentment on his face. When she is gone, he digs back into his work.

As the clock strikes six, Megumi finds herself approaching a quaint little ramen restaurant nestled in the heart of Kanda. This older, slightly worn-down area of Tokyo pulsates with life, resonating with the hum of tourists and locals alike relishing their typical Friday night. The golden glow from the restaurant windows spills onto the pavement, painting a warm picture against the evening backdrop. On reaching, she spots Kazu in the alley next to the establishment, his silhouette illuminated by a lone lamplight. He is puffing on a cigarette, the smoke twirling upwards in the chilly air, his gaze keen and vigilant, scanning the area with an air of alertness not common for the casual observer. He notices Megumi approaching and he casually drops his cigarette, gives her a smile and walks over to her. They both enter the small restaurant.

Upon entering the cozy ramen shop, Kazu and Megumi navigate to one of the small tables tucked in the back corner, a spot offering a modicum of privacy amidst the bustling atmosphere. Almost immediately, the shop owner, an elderly man with a face etched with the lines of time and experience, spots Kazu. He ambles over, his face breaking into a smile of recognition. Kazu orders a cold beer, the condensation on the bottle reflecting the dim light of the room. Megumi opts for a sparkling water, adding with a light laugh that the wedding is merely two weeks away, and she is on a mission to look her slimmest in her wedding dress. They both order ramen, the quintessential comfort food, a fitting choice for the easy camaraderie that fills the air.

Meanwhile, across the city in another pulsating district of Tokyo, Ryan is engaged in a rigorous Jiu-Jitsu training session. He and his training partner, Hiroshi, a burly Japanese man in his late twenties, are locked in an intense sparring match. Beneath the harsh fluorescent lights of the dojo, their bodies twist and turn, grapple and grip; each seeking to gain dominance, to pin the other down, to achieve the victorious hold of submission. They roll on the mat like two combatants, their Jiu-Jitsu gi's slick with sweat, their breaths coming in ragged gasps, their muscles straining with the effort of the fight. The dojo echoes with the sound of their grunts of exertion, the slap of skin against skin, the sharp exhale of breath. But neither man can gain the upper hand, their skill levels are too closely matched. The stalemate continues, neither willing to back down, their determination fueling their efforts as they relentlessly pursue victory. Ryan gets mounted on top of Hiroshi and extends his arm and Hiroshi taps vigorously for Ryan to stop. Ryan lets go and rolls off to the side of Hiroshi. Hiroshi sits up and gives Ryan a congratulatory tap on his chest, "Nice move my friend." Ryan, still out of breath sits up and looks to Hiroshi, "I got lucky. You nearly had me so many times." They both sit on the mat, trying to catch their breath, sweat dripping from their faces. A long moment passes and Hiroshi smiles, "I think professor is giving you your Black Belt tonight." Ryan shakes his head, "Not a chance my friend, not a chance."

Moments later, the dojo falls silent as the instructor, a lean and stern man with a lifetime of martial arts etched into his face, calls everyone to line up to end the class. As the row of sweaty, disciplined students form a line, the instructor begins to talk. His voice, calm and authoritative, cuts through the lingering tension in the room. Mid-speech, he pauses and turns his gaze towards Ryan. "Ryan," he beckons, "Please, step forward." A wave of surprise sweeps over Ryan as he slowly rises to his feet and walks towards the instructor. The room is hushed now, every eye fixed on Ryan. He reaches the instructor and kneels in front of him. The instructor, holding Ryan's gaze for a moment, reaches into his uniform top and pulls out a folded black belt. The room erupts in applause as Ryan reluctantly stands up and outstretches his arms as his instructor ties the crisp, new Black Belt around his waist.

As Ryan stands in front of the class, his fellow students are clapping with an enthusiasm that nearly moves him to tears. Years of training, sweat and perseverance brought him to this point and he cannot help but draw the correlation to this, as well as the success in his love life. So many times, so many setbacks only to feel despair and doubt turn to utter joy. Life could simply not be any better.

Now we are back in the Ramen restaurant.

At the Ramen restaurant, the atmosphere is markedly different. Kazu and Megumi sit opposite each other, a stark contrast to the jovial celebration at the dojo. Tension is palpable in the air, their faces tight with unease. In front of Kazu lies an array of empty beer glasses, a futile attempt to lighten the mood, while the untouched ramen bowls in front of them slowly cool down. Their eyes meet, the casual conversation they've been trying to keep up suddenly falls silent. Megumi looks at Kazu, her gaze heavy with a mix of uncertainty and concern, as she braces herself to break the silence. "So they have been attacking your clubs? I still don't understand why? There has been a truce for more than five years?"

Kazu nods, a look of grave concern on his face. "The crackdowns in Osaka have pushed their group into Tokyo. They don't want to see their earnings slow down."

Megumi nods pensively, "You need to get out. You need to quit. Immediately." Kazu looks at her incredulously and chuckles. He scans the room to see if anybody is listening in. When he is comfortable that they are not, he grins at Megumi. "And do what? This is all I have ever done. I have no job history and no skills."

Megumi is the consummate deal maker. She is undeterred, "What would you like to do? I can help you. You can come work at our company?"

Kazu raises his empty beer glass to the shop owner. The shop owner nods and begins to fill him another glass of beer. Kazu looks back to Megumi, "That's really nice of you, but I don't have any other skills. Unless you want me to run your collections department?"

Megumi presses on, "You have skills. More skills than half of my current employees. You're a great communicator, and a great negotiator. You are very charismatic and you are good under pressure. I can find a spot in our company."

The shop owner brings over the fresh beer. Kazu lifts his glass to Megumi, "I negotiate with a short sword and my fists. Not too sure your board will like my style." Megumi takes a long pause, "I won't tell them. You can work with Ryan in the marketing department."

Kazu shakes his head, "There are laws against hiring Yakuza. You know that. You will get yourself in serious trouble." Megumi gives him a look of steely eyed determination, "You think that you are the only one who breaks the law? You're my brother, and you are telling me that a gang war is going to break out. I need to get you out of that group. Now."

Kazu just looks at her, "I'm not a coward. I am not afraid to die."

Megumi's head drops as she gazes into her untouched ramen. Tears welling in her eyes. She looks up at Kazu, tears welling up in her eyes, "For years, I pretended you didn't exist. Didn't want you to exist. I know what you did for Ryan. How you saved him. If not for you stepping in, he would have been dead. Ryan is my life. And you saved him. I am forever in debt to you. Please let me do this one thing. Let met get you out."

Kazu rubs his forehead. It's not CEO and Yakuza here talking. It is simply brother and sister. Megumi notices a text from Ryan. She picks up her phone, opens it and smiles. She holds the phone up for Kazu to see. It's Ryan, with his classmates at Jiu-Jitsu, showing off his new Black Belt. Kazu nods and forces a smile.

Megumi puts a cap on their dinner in the same way she would wrap up one of her weekly executive meetings, "I need to get home. By tomorrow I will send you a few different roles you can take in our company. Let me know which fits you best. You can start next week."

Kazu looks at Megumi with a really unique mix of resignation and gratitude. Even a bit of pride. He has never held a legit job. A job that he could tell people about with pride. Thoughts went through his head of living a normal life, with an upstanding job. Sure, people around Tokyo show him respect, but it's more respect out of fear. This would be respect that he is contributing to society, rather than taking from it.

Years of reading people in a professional setting have clearly paid off for Megumi. She studies him and she can tell that she just changed his life in a big way. She cracks a smile and reaches across the table and puts her hand on top of his. She looks into his eyes, "You're my brother. And

I love you."

He nods. Tears are welling up in his eyes, but he wills them away, "I just don't want to let you down. What if I fail?" The tough and arrogant Yakuza has faded away. Now he is just a little boy, trapped in a young man's body looking at his sister. All varnish of posturing has been stripped away. Megumi gives him a look now that unless you knew, you would think she is the hard scrabble gangster.

"You will do fine. Trust me. The only way you let me down is if you don't accept my offer. Are you going to let me down?" She adds dryly, "You're not going to let me down, right?"

Silently, he shakes his head no. If he spoke right now, he would cry. He was not going to let that happen.

CHAPTER FORTY-SEVEN

Breaking the News

As Megumi entered her home, the familiar hum of the city at night was replaced by the quiet tranquility of her living room. There, on the couch, sat Ryan, her eyes sparkling with excitement. Almost instantly, his enthusiasm dimmed, replaced by confusion at the sight of Megumi's somber expression.

"Hey, I've got some good news," he started, standing up to greet her, the excitement in his voice barely contained. "I got my black belt tonight!"

But his words hung in the air, intercepted by the serious look on Megumi's face. The joy in his eyes was quickly replaced by concern. It was clear to him, even before she spoke, that something significant had happened, something that would overshadow his news. He sat back down, the telltale sign of a black belt forgotten, his attention fully on Megumi. "What's wrong?" he asked, the room growing heavy with anticipation.

Forcing a smile onto her face, Megumi looked at Ryan and said, "That's great, Ryan. I'm really proud of you," as genuine warmth seeped into her words. Yet, her strained voice and the tight lines around her eyes betrayed her feigned enthusiasm. Seeing this, Ryan's concern deepened.

"What's going on?" he insisted, his excitement over his achievement completely evaporating now. He knew her too well. Something was definitely up, and it wasn't something good. Ryan presses on, "Did things go bad at dinner?" Megumi takes a deep breath, "Kazu.. he needs to come work at the company."

Ryan is confused, "So.. things went good it sounds like?"

Megumi gathers her thoughts as Ryan studies her expression, "There are some things happening, in Kazu's work, that he needs to get out. Immediately."

Ryan continues to look at her. He is still confused. She continues, "Another group is moving into Tokyo. It's going to lead to trouble. Big trouble. They are hitting their nightclubs and street vendors and wanting to take over."

"So he's going to quit and come work at our company?" Ryan asks. Megumi nods. Ryan's expression turns from concern to happiness and relief, "That's awesome. What is he going to do? I think that's a great thing?"

"You won't be upset?" Megumi asks. "Upset? No, I think it's great. I think he would be a great fit." Ryan replies instantly. "What is he going to do?" Ryan asks, clearly excited about the prospect of his soon to be brother in law working with them, side by side.

Megumi takes a deep breath. The stress of dinner and the heavy conversation fading away like the last rays of the sun on a romantic sunset. She smiles, "I feel so much better, I'm relieved you're not upset. I gave him a few options of things he can do. Maybe marketing with you, maybe product testing, I am not really sure yet. I am going to email him some job descriptions."

Ryan smiles, "Marketing, with me. I can move out of my office and down to the cubicles. I can teach him anything he needs to know. I think that's great."

Megumi pulls in close and gives him a soft kiss, "Thank you. For everything. For understanding, for supporting me in this. Thank you for everything. I love you so much."

He gives her another kiss, "I love you too."

She pulls back and playfully slaps him on the chest lightly, "But no way you are moving down to the cubicles. I would miss you too much. Plus, I want to make sure you are not talking to any of the other girls."

He grins, "I would never.." She laughs, "Maybe you wouldn't talk with them, but they would talk with you, and then I would have to fire more people. You know I am protective like that."

Ryan drops a question, "But Kazu, he can just quit the Yakuza?" Megumi raises her eyebrows, "I hope so. I may have to pay them off.." Ryan nods. He understands enough to know that the Yakuza isn't something one can just quit with an email giving two weeks notice.

Megumi looks to Ryan, "I'm starving, have you eaten?" He grins, "I thought you and Kazu had dinner? And no, I have not eaten." She takes a deep breath, "We didn't really eat, let's go out."

Just then, she gets a text. She looks at it and smiles with pride. She holds the phone up for Ryan to see, "He just accepted. Wants my advice on books he can read over the weekend so he can be prepared. I think he's really excited. A bit nervous though." Ryan chuckles, "Marketing, with me. Tell him that I have him covered one hundred percent. I'm moving to the cubicles."

She shakes her head with fake exasperation, "You are definitely not moving to the cubicles. Let's go."

They chuckle and smile as they make their way to the door.

CHAPTER FORTY-EIGHT

The New Guy

Ryan stood waiting in the sleek lobby of the office building, nervously checking his watch. The double glass doors swished open, and in walked Kazu, looking every bit as anxious as he felt.

"Good morning, Kazu," Ryan greeted, extending a hand, "Welcome to your first day."

Kazu took the hand, nodding, "Thank you, Ryan-san."

Ryan smiled, "No need for formalities, Kazu. We are practically family. I understand it's a big transition for you, but we're here to support you."

Kazu looked around at the bustling office space, taking in the sight of his new professional life. He took a deep breath. Ryan noticed his apprehension.

Ryan patted his shoulder reassuringly, "I know it's a pretty big change, but I have you covered. Anything you need. Okay?"

Their conversation was interrupted by a friendly voice. "Hey, you two should probably get moving before I fire you both."

They turned to see Megumi, grinning broadly at them. Ryan rolled his eyes at her, but Kazu just seemed relieved at her friendly demeanor.

"Come on," Ryan said, leading the way towards the elevators, "Let's get you settled in. Welcome aboard."

As the elevator doors shut, leaving Kazu and Ryan to start their new journey together, Kazu couldn't help but feel a spark of excitement amidst the nerves. It was his first taste of a legitimate profession and he liked it a lot. He would definitely give his all to impress his new colleagues.

The elevator doors glide open and Ryan and Kazu make their way through the cubicles. The other employees take note of Kazu, a new face in the room. Ryan, brimming with his usual confidence and charisma stops at some of the cubicles to introduce the new employee, and it's clear that Ryan is doing his best to make the new hire feel at home.

After the obligatory introductions, Ryan and Kazu finally make it over to Kazu's cubicle. Ryan looks to Kazu, "Here we are. Here's your desk." Kazu flashes Ryan a tentative smile before sitting down at his desk. He runs his fingers over the desk and laptop, taking it all in. He notices the name plate on the corner, it reads "Kazue Sato, Marketing" in both Japanese and English. Ryan studies Kazu's reaction and smiles. Kazu notices Ryan's caring and thoughtful look and smiles back, "Thank you. I really appreciate this. I have a lot to learn, but I promise I will do my best to not let you down." Ryan nods before giving Kazu a comforting pat on the shoulder, "I know. You're going to do great."

Ryan made his way down the plush hallway on the executive floor to his own office. Once inside, he settled comfortably into his plush chair, the familiar surroundings a stark contrast to Kazu's newness. Moments later, Megumi walked into Ryan's office, her eyes radiating concern. "How's his first day going?" she asked, leaning against the doorframe. "Is he nervous?" Ryan looked up from his screen, a thoughtful expression crossing his face as he considered Megumi's inquiry. Ryan nods, "A bit, but I think he will be great." Megumi smiles softly, "Thank you. For everything. I really appreciate you looking after him." Ryan nods, "Of course."

As the mid-day sun bathed the city in a warm glow, the office atmosphere started to wind down, signaling the much-awaited lunch break. Ryan, true to his supportive nature, decided it was the perfect opportunity to further acquaint Kazu with his new environment. He strolled over to Kazu's cubicle, a friendly smile on his face. "Lunch?" he asked, leaning against the cubicle wall. Kazu looked up from his work, his face lighting up at the invite. "Yes, that would be great," he replied enthusiastically. Ryan nodded, and the two men stood up, leaving the office together, their easy camaraderie blending well with the bustling cityscape outside.

Ryan and Kazu are eating lunch in a small ramen shop that is surprisingly deserted, despite it being lunch time. Ryan looks to Kazu with legitimate care, "How's the first day? Getting settled in?" Kazu nods, "Going okay." Ryan notices the hesitation, "Yeah? Any issues?" Kazu shakes his head, "No." Ryan is not convinced, "You seem.. I don't know?" Kazu takes a deep breath, "It is all just so new. Sitting at a desk, sending emails. Filling things out. Just a big change." Ryan raises his eyebrows, he can relate. "Yeah, I know it's a lot. People are being good to you though right?" Kazu nods. Ryan continues, "When we get back to the office, why don't you come up with me and I can walk you through some of the material, so you can get familiar with it?" Kazu flashes Ryan a sincere look of appreciation.

As the glow of the setting sun filtered through the blinds of Ryan's office window, casting a warm hue over the room, the door creaked open. Megumi peered in, her eyes softening when she found Ryan still engrossed in his work. "Ready to head home?" she asked gently, leaning against the doorframe. At her voice, Ryan glanced up, a soft sigh escaping his lips as he nodded, quickly packing away his laptop in his bag.

They left his office together, their footsteps echoing in the near-empty office. As they walked past Kazu's cubicle, they found him still engrossed in his work, his focus riveted on his computer screen. The surrounding cubicles were deserted, their occupants having left for the day, but Kazu was still there, putting in extra hours to familiarize himself with his new role. The sight tugged at Ryan's heartstrings, reinforcing his resolve to support Kazu through his transition.

Ryan and Megumi walk over to Kazu's cubicle, unnoticed. Ryan gives a slight knock on the cubicle wall and Kazu looks up, slightly started, "You ready to take off?" Ryan asks. Kazu rubs his eyes for a moment, "Almost. Just want to get through this last thing you sent me." Ryan chuckles, "It can wait. You have put in a really long day. Why don't you take off with us?" Kazu looks over to Megumi, who is smiling at her brother with a pride and appreciation that warms his heart. Ryan persists, "Let's go. It will still be here tomorrow." Kazu nods and looks around the cubicle, "Okay to leave this stuff here? Do I need to take it with me?" Ryan shakes his head, "Maybe just take your laptop? Everything else is cool to leave here."

With that, Kazu grabs the laptop, drops it into his backpack and readies to leave.

Megumi, Ryan and Kazu are standing just outside of the massive office building. The streets are pulsing with activity and Kazu seems drawn to it, rejuvenated as he scans the surroundings. It's clear that he is Yakuza, and even though he was trapped in a cubicle all day, he is a man of the streets. Megumi takes note, "Join us for dinner?" Kazu looks distracted as he replies, "Thank you, maybe not tonight though. I have some errands to run."

Kazu turns his look to Ryan, "I want to thank you for today. I know you are busy, but you took so much time to help me. I promise I will be better tomorrow." Ryan is surprised, "You did great. I didn't really do anything." Kazu smiles. He is truly grateful. With that, Kazu smiles and nods at Ryan and Megumi and walks off, melting into the group of passersby on the sidewalk and off into the night. Ryan looks to Megumi, "You ready?" She smiles and nods and they head the other way, onto the crowded street.

It's late at night and Ryan and Megumi's penthouse is completely silent, save for the sound of a running shower coming from their bathroom. Ryan is standing in the shower, letting the hot water run over him in a relaxing wave. His eyes are closed and he is lost in thought when he feels a hand on his shoulder. He opens his eyes and looks over to see Megumi touching his shoulder. She has a seductive and serious look in her eyes, "I am looking very forward to being your wife." He is taken aback, "I can't wait too." She caresses his face and shoulders, the same faraway look in her eyes, "You don't understand, you are the only man I have ever loved, the only man I could ever love." Ryan smiles, "I feel the same about you." She continues, "The way you look after Kazu, you're very caring. You are truly one of a kind." He's not sure what to say, "Of course, he's your brother. I will do anything for him." She just nods, "I want you. Come to bed with me?" Their eyes lock and he nods.

An hour has passed, and Ryan and Megumi are laying in bed. Ryan is reading a book, while Megumi gently glides her fingers across Ryan's bare chest. "Two weeks. I will be your wife. I hope that we never change." Ryan dips the book and looks to her, "It'll be perfect. Nothing is going to change." She smiles wistfully, "I hope not."

As the two lovers lay in bed, the gears of fate continue to turn. Neither could imagine just how different life would be in just two short weeks.

Chapter Forty-Nine

Time Stand Still

In the heart of the city, far above the bustling streets below, Ryan sits in his office. It's late Friday afternoon, and the waning sunlight paints the room with a warm, golden hue. His eyes are fixated on his computer screen, fingers dancing swiftly across the keyboard as he works to finish up a crucial project.

Suddenly, the office door swings open and Megumi steps in. She's wearing a radiant smile that complements the soft glow of the setting sun, and her presence immediately fills the room. "Ready?" she asks softly, leaning against the door frame. His eyes flit away from his screen and meet hers - they sparkle with affection and a hint of exhaustion. "Just wrapping up a few things," he replies.

With a glance at the clock on Ryan's desk, Megumi crosses her arms and raises an eyebrow. "You know, we have our final meeting with the wedding planners today. And you promised we would leave together." Her voice is playful yet firm, and Ryan can't help but smile. "I know, I know," he says, hitting save on his work and shutting his computer down.

Ryan swiftly gathers his belongings, standing up from his desk and joining Megumi at the door. As they exit the office together, Ryan gives Megumi a smile and stops. He looks into her eyes and she freezes. "You okay?" She asks. Ryan nods, still looking deeply into her eyes. "We need to get going, or we are going to be late." She continues. Ryan takes her hand and peers deeply into her eyes. "Take this moment. Let's never forget it." There is something in the way he says it that makes her heart skip a beat, Ryan continues. "I love you, more than life itself. I have loved you since the moment I first saw you." Her pulse quickens and she is at a loss for words. After a long pause she smiles. "We need to get going." With that, he nods and they leave. As they leave the office, something feels different to Megumi. She wonders why his sudden intensity came about. As she works to figure it out, she realizes that she just fell in love with Ryan all over again.

In the elegantly furnished office of their wedding planner, Ryan and Megumi sit across from the planner, reviewing the final details of their upcoming nuptials. The soft hum of conversation fills the room as every aspect of their special day is confirmed - from the venue to the flowers, the menu, and the guest list. The planner, with her practiced smile, assures them, "All your plans are confirmed."

Ryan nods in acknowledgment, his hand reaching into his pocket to pull out a check. It's the final payment for both the wedding venue and the planner's diligent service. He hands it over to the planner, his relaxed demeanor belying the weight of the moment. This final transaction is symbolic, representing the end of their planning journey and the beginning of a new chapter, one filled with love, commitment, and an endless future together.

As the planner tucks away the check, Megumi turns to Ryan, her eyes sparkling in the dim light. "How about we celebrate the end of our planning with a dinner out?" she suggests, her voice a soft whisper. Ryan, always keen on Megumi's suggestions, readily agrees. "A great idea," he affirms, his gaze steady on Megumi. Their exchange of smiles, filled with unspoken love, is a testament to their shared excitement for their future. With that, they rise from the plush chairs, hand in hand, and step out of the planner's office. As the door closes behind them, they are encompassed by the tranquility of the night. The stars, a silent witness to their love story, twinkle in approval as they make their way to a nearby restaurant, known for its exquisite menu and elegant ambience, to celebrate the successful completion of a key life event.

As they settle into their seats in the elegant restaurant, the soft ambient music providing a calming backdrop, Megumi breaks the comfortable silence between them. She looks at Ryan with a curious smile, her fingers lightly tracing the rim of her wine glass. "Ryan," she starts, her voice filled with curiosity, "back in the office, you told me that we should never forget that moment. What brought that on?" Ryan, surprised by her astuteness, takes a moment to compose his thoughts. Taking a sip from his glass, he meets her gaze, his eyes reflecting the sincerity of his feelings. "I guess in that moment," he begins, his voice barely above a whisper, "handing over that check, I realized how real all of this is – our wedding, our future. It wasn't just about affirming my love for you, but also acknowledging how ready I am ready to start the rest of my life with you." His heartfelt confession is met with Megumi's understanding smile, a testament to the deep bond they share. She presses on, "It just felt.. like there was something more to it?" Ryan nods, suddenly pensive, "Do you know what I love most about our lives together?" She takes a sip of wine from her glass. She gives him a curious look as he continues, "It's the little things. Just seeing you in the hallway, I feel like a kid again, with butterflies in my stomach. When I am in my office working, I think about you. You're twenty feet away in your office, and I still miss you. Any time I am away from you, I just feel like part of me is missing." There it is again, his words so raw, and so accurate. Her pulse quickens.

She says, "The day when you were flying back from Los Angeles.." She stops and he nods solemnly. She works to gather her precise words to describe it, "I thought you were gone, that I would never see you again. I have never felt so lost in my entire life." Her words hang over the table with an indescribable weight. She runs her elegant index finger around the rim of her wine glass as she looks down at it. Ryan senses the moment and reaches across the table and takes her hand.

Their dinner is complete and they exit the restaurant. Megumi looks to Ryan, "Take a walk along the river?" Ryan nods, "You read my mind." They stroll off down the street towards the path that lines the Sumida River.

Ryan and Megumi are strolling down the path that lines the river. The scene is perfect, as the river flows gently, each small wave crest reflecting the elegant lights of the Tokyo skyline. A gentle breeze is blowing, filled with the smells of nearby restaurants. Megumi walks over to the railing and peers out over the water. She speaks to Ryan as she gazes out over the water with a wistful look. "I dream of that same thing too." Ryan takes his spot along the railing, standing closely beside her. "What's that?" He asks. "For time to stand still." She continues. He just nods, it's unspoken. Their life and romance together has been so whirlwind, and faced so many hurdles and obstacles initially, that they both want to just take a break and savor the moment. Each struggle with a gnawing feeling that there is always something just off on the horizon that can put an end to their beautiful lives together.

Almost on cue, a man approaches as Ryan and Megumi are gazing off at the water, just savoring the moment. Ryan looks over and instantly recognizes him. It is the young Yakuza that Ryan laid the beating on just outside of their office a while back. As he approaches, Ryan turns to face the man, instinctively stepping in front of Megumi. With a calm, yet firm voice Ryan greets him, "Hey, what's up?

Without speaking, the young Yakuza comes up and stands looking at Ryan, and then over at Megumi and back to Ryan without saying a word. Ryan just looks at him, ready to spring back into action if needed. The young Yakuza surveys the situation and after a long moment he speaks. "I hear you're getting married, congratulations." His words are nice, but they are delivered with a sneer and cocky grin that don't really align. Ryan nods, still tense, "Thank you." The Yakuza nods and looks around, surveying the area, "I need you to come with me."

Normally, Ryan would be asking questions where they would be going and why, but deep down Ryan knows why. The gang wars have been escalating badly over the past month and this man's organization, and Kazu's former organization, have been getting decimated. Kazu has been keeping Ryan updated on the happenings and shared that their boss has been trying hard to get Kazu back on the streets to defend their holdings. Megumi is shocked with Ryan nods in agreement. Ryan turns to face Megumi, "It will be fine, let me get you a car." Megumi shakes her head, "I don't want a car. I just want us to go home... together. You have no business going with him." Ryan places his hands on Megumi's shoulders, "It will be fine. Trust me. Let me get you a car." Something in the way Ryan says it makes her understand that he is going, no matter how much she is against it. She nods.

It is just minutes later and a black town car arrives and Megumi gets in after she delivers a quick kiss on Ryan's cheek. As the car pulls away into the night, she looks out the back window at Ryan and the young Yakuza as they walk off towards an unknown location.

Megumi says a silent prayer for his safety, knowing that if anything happens to Ryan her life would simply cease to matter.

CHAPTER FIFTY

Ishida

Ryan slides into the back seat of a large, black town car, the leather cool and smooth against his skin. The young Yakuza member slips into the driver's seat with practiced ease. His hands move with an ingrained familiarity over the controls, adjusting the mirrors slightly before he starts the engine, the low purr of the car filling the otherwise silent night.

"Your phone," The young Yakuza commands, not taking his eyes off the road. Ryan complies without a word, handing over his phone. The device disappears into the man's jacket pocket, leaving Ryan with nothing but his own thoughts to occupy the journey. The car glides forward, merging seamlessly with the night, its destination unknown. The city lights turn into a blur as they recede in the rearview mirror, replaced by the inky darkness that lies ahead. The silence in the car is punctuated only by the steady rhythm of the tires against the asphalt, a dirge marching them deeper into an uncertain fate.

Some thirty or so minutes have passed and Ryan leans forward, "Can you please tell me where you are going?" The young Yakuza peers into the rear view mirror so he can make eye contact with Ryan, "Relax. You're safe." Ryan persists, "Yes, but where are we going." The young Yakuza ignores Ryan's question and continues to drive.

The black town car winds its way along a dark, thickly forested two lane road. They are deep in the countryside, only periodic dots of lights from rural estates interrupt the darkness.

Abruptly, the car turns off of the road and onto a long, tree lined driveway.

The estate that now comes into view is a striking blend of contemporary and traditional Japanese architecture, a testament to the elegant harmony of old and new. The grand entrance, framed by meticulously manicured bonsai trees, leads to a sprawling, single-story structure that redefines luxury. The exterior is adorned with distinctive attributes of traditional Japanese design - wooden facades, sliding doors, and a gently sloping roof with broad eaves. Yet, these elements are seamlessly integrated with modern, minimalist aesthetics. Floor-to-ceiling glass walls and sleek steel frames coexist with intricate woodwork, creating an elegant juxtaposition that suggests both opulence and restraint. Subtle lighting illuminates the estate, casting soft shadows on the surrounding garden and reflecting off the tranquil koi pond — a staple of Japanese landscaping. The house, while undoubtedly expensive, exudes a quiet, understated grandeur that echoes the serene ambiance of the surrounding countryside.

The car pulls to a stop and Ryan gets out. The young Yakuza rolls down the window and nods to Ryan, "You can go in." Ryan looks up to the home and back to the man peering back at him. The Yakuza nods, "It's safe. You're expected." Ryan takes another long look at the home and back to the man, "Thanks for the ride.. and not killing me." This time the Yakuza smiles, not the usual sneer, but an authentic smile. He gives a chuckle, "No problem. Thanks for being a good passenger." Ryan nods, "And for what it's worth, I am sorry for the other day." With that, the young Yakuza hands Ryan his phone back, "Here, call me when you are done. I will drive you back."

Relief washes over Ryan. He knows that there will be a return trip. Up until now, he was not sure if he would be alive for a ride home. There is something in their conversation that makes Ryan sort of like him. In a bizarre thought, he wonders what was this young man's life path that brought him to the Yakuza life. Ryan asks, "I don't have your number." The young guy smiles and hands him his business card. "Here." Ryan accepts it and walks over to the home.

As Ryan makes it to the porch, he is greeted by the boss. The older Yakuza looks very different from the time Ryan last saw him. He seems older, tired and even a bit vulnerable. Now, he does not so imposing, and he could easily be mistaken for an aging sushi chef, or even a dock work-er. He extends his hand to shake and Ryan accepts. The boss looks at Ryan and adds, "I don't normally shake hands. Consider that a welcome to my home. My name is Ishida.. Kenji Ishida. Thank you for coming." Ryan nods and bows slightly, "Mr. Ishida, nice to meet you.. formally."

Ishida nods, "Please come in." Ryan nods and they enter the home. They make their way through the home and into a well appointed living room. A moment later, Ishida's wife Mayu approaches with a tray carry-ing a beautiful, dark blue ceramic pot of green tea. Two empty tea cups as well. As steam gently wafts from the ceramic pot, Ryan is drawn to the design on the pot. It's dark blue, almost midnight blue and is dotted with a pattern that looks like stars in the night. Mayu nods as she sets the tray down in front of the two, who are seated on a large overstuffed leather couch.

Ishida looks to Mayu, and back to Ryan, "This is my wife Mayu." She smiles and bows slightly and Ryan does the same. As Ryan looks at Mayu, he is taken by her elegant beauty. She is in her early sixties, but her skin is flawless. Ryan has to ask himself in wonder at the things she has seen being married to Ishida. Mayu leaves after another slight bow. Ryan watches as she gracefully glides from the room. As soon as she leaves, Ishida turns his gaze back to Ryan, "I am a direct descendant of the Hojo clan. They were samurai dating back to the twelve hundreds.." Ryan interrupts, ".. and were direct retainers of the Kamakura Shogunate. The Hojo were every bit as powerful as the Tokugawa." Ishida stops in his tracks and looks at Ryan, peering deeply into his eyes with surprise. Ryan stops, it was rude for him to interrupt such a proud and powerful man. Ishida nods, "I can see you know your Japanese history. Impressive. But then, as you may or may not know, my family had our power stripped by the Toyotomi in fifteen-ninety. They lost their power and were sent away." Again, Ryan interrupts, ".. and Hojo and his wife were sent away to Mount Koya. Hojo's wife was actually Tokugawa Iyeyasu's daughter, right?" Ishida is visibly shocked. Ryan holds up his hand slightly with a nod to apologize. Ishida nods, "How do you know this? Did you study this in school?" Ryan looks down at his tea and back up to Ishida, "When I fell in love with Megumi she pushed me away. She said that she could not be with her because we were too different. So I wanted to learn more about her.. and her culture." With this, Ishida laughs loudly, "You learned about Japanese feudalism because you wanted a Japanese woman? That is crazy." Ryan chuckles, "Maybe, but I knew that even if she didn't love me, I would love her... and I would spend the rest of my life changing her mind." With this, something clicks inside of Ishida and he gave Ryan an almost fatherly look.

Ishida sighs deeply. He takes a sip of the still hot green tea and looks to Ryan, "I have grown up in this organization, just like my father, and his father before him. It has been my life. In nineteen eighty nine, I was put in control of this organization, to not only preserve it, but to grow it. Things are slipping away and if I cannot fix it, I will end up in exile..

just like the Hojo. We all will."

Although not understanding where this is going, Ryan still nods. He was about to find out.

Ishida looks to Ryan with a steely eyed resolve, "The reason I called you here is because you can fix it. I am afraid that you are the only one who can."

Ryan, confused, "Fix it? Me?"

Ishida nods and takes a photo out from an inner pocket of his kimono and hands it to Ryan, "I need you to kill this man." Before looking at the photo, Ryan asks, "Kill him?" Ishida nods, his eyes filled with a cold calm, "This is the leader of the group pushing us out. You need to kill him and they will retreat. Preserving our place in Tokyo." Thoughts rush through Ryan's head as he looks at this man's photo. This is exactly what Megumi had feared.. what she had warned him about. Ryan sits frozen, looking at the black and white photo. Ishida continues, "You will be given instructions and an unregistered weapon that day."

Ryan tries to remain calm, but inside he is gripped with a whirlwind of fear and questions, "You want me to kill him? But I will get caught, and I will go to prison?" Ishida shakes his head, "The police don't know you. They will not suspect you."

Ryan fires back, "You can't ask me to kill somebody. I am not a killer." Ishida leans forward, "I am not asking. I am telling. You made me a pact, on your honor, that you owed me. You said you would do anything. This is how you will repay me."

Ishida can read the fear in Ryan's eyes. He gives Ryan a knowing look, "Kazu-san told me that would be your reaction. He volunteered to take your place." Ryan is confused, "Kazu?" Ishida nods, "Kazu-san fought hard to step in for you. He knew this would be your reaction. I made a promise to Kazu's father that I would let him leave the Yakuza and I intend to honor it."

Ryan sits on the couch dumbfounded. Thoughts racing through his mind. He had to find a way out of it. There is no way he can go home and tell Megumi about this. Ishida sits looking at Ryan for a long moment before speaking, "This is something you have to do. This is your duty. Once completed, I will be forever in your debt. You, Megumi, and any future children you have. You will always be under our protection. I give you my promise."

Ryan nods with resignation, "Okay. I will do it. When? How?" Ishida flashes a knowing grin, "The plans will be given to you, but it will be next Saturday, the day of your wedding. In the time after your ceremony, and before your flight leaves for your honeymoon. You will get on a plane and leave for two weeks and by the time you return to Tokyo, all will have passed. Your alibi and lack of police record will keep you safe."

For a brief moment, Ryan had to be impressed with Ishida's logic and strategy. It only lasted a moment though before the stark reality hit him that yes, Ishida was not asking and the only way that Ryan makes it back alive tonight, or much less to their actual wedding day is if he does this.

Ryan nods, "Okay." With this, Ishida stands up and looks to Ryan, "I wish I did not come to this, but there is no other way. It's late, I need to go to sleep. Have a safe drive back to the city. We will be in touch."

Ryan takes his cue and stands up. Ishida leaves the room and Mayu enters, walking Ryan to the door without saying a word.

Ryan steps out into the night to find the black town car waiting to take him back to the city.

CHAPTER FIFTY-ONE
Soul Search

As the black town car hummed its way back to Tokyo, Ryan found himself sinking deeper into the leather backseat, the rhythmic vibrations of the road lulling his body into a false sense of calm that his mind sharply rejected. The young Yakuza at the wheel occasionally glanced at Ryan through the rearview mirror, his expression inscrutable yet tinged with a shadow of understanding. The city's neon skyline slowly painted itself against the night as they approached, each light a beacon of normalcy, of lives untouched by the weight of a promise such as the one Ryan had been ensnared in. But the garish brightness didn't reach inside the car, where Ryan was left alone with his thoughts, each twist and turn of the road seeming to echo the turmoil within him.

The cityscape raced by in a blur, but inside the town car, time seemed to slow as Ryan grappled with the enormity of his task. He was no assassin; he was a man swept up in the undertow of Ishida's influence, a man who protected and nurtured Megumi and Kazu when they needed him the most. The knot in his chest tightened at the thought of her. How could he face Megumi, his beacon of light, and confess that the shadow of the Yakuza had crept into their lives, demanding a deed so dark? The whispers of the car's wheels seemed to mock him, offering no answers, only amplifying the silent scream in his head. As the car snaked through the labyrinth of Tokyo's outskirts, Ryan felt the crushing isolation of his predicament. No matter the turns he took, the dead end was the same: fulfill Ishida's grim directive, or forfeit everything he held dear.

The silence stretched between them, a palpable presence in the cold leather confines of the car. Then, unexpectedly, the young Yakuza's gaze caught Ryan's in the rearview once more, but this time something was different, a flicker of something like empathy in his otherwise stoic eyes. He turned fully, the engines hum a low background to his words. "Thank you," he said, his voice oddly gentle for someone of his standing, "I know it's not easy. My first one was too." His words, heavily laced with an uncharacteristic kindness, seemed to hang in the air, and for a brief moment, the gap between their worlds felt infinitesimally smaller. Ryan just looks at him, their eyes locked in a stare in the rear view mirror. The young Yakuza continues, "For what it's worth, I wish I could be the one to do it." Ryan breaks his silence after a long pause, "I know."

After what felt like an eternity, the black town car arrives outside of Ryan and Megumi's luxury high rise. Ryan hesitates to get out. After a long moment, he realizes that he cannot avoid this. He has to go upstairs and tell Megumi everything. Once resigned, he gets out of the car. As he gets out, the window glides down and the young Yakuza calls out to him, "Oy." Ryan turns to look before walking back to the car and looking in through the open window. The young Yakuza hands Ryan a business card, "You're with us now. You have no problems. If you have a problem, you tell me, or you tell Oyabun and we will handle it." The sincerity in his voice and the look in his eye is somehow comforting. Ryan accepts the card with a nod, "Thank you."

The car drives out into the night. Ryan watches as it merges into traffic. As he stands, his mind is a tornado of emotion. Just moments ago, he could not see himself taking another person's life - at least not in such a cold and calculated way. Now, in a bizarre turn of events, it all is making sense to him. He thinks back to Ishida, with his polished and charismatic demeanor, and he understands why he is the boss of the Tokyo underworld. Ryan looks at the business card handed to him moments ago. It's only a business card, but the meaning and significance it represents makes it feel immeasurably heavy and, in a twisted sort of way, treasured. As he tucks the card into his pocket, he is beginning to understand how someone can end up in the Yakuza. It's an intoxicating mix of power, prestige and history. However, membership in this club has heavy dues, and Ryan's will need to pay his soon.

He pulls his cell phone from his pocket and turns it on. Multiple text messages come flooding in from Megumi checking to see if he is okay. He types a quick reply and quickly makes his way into the building.

Ryan steps into the luxury apartment he shares with Megumi, the polished floors and sleek lines a stark contrast to the night's chaotic events. No sooner had the door clicked shut behind him than Megumi rushes towards him. She wraps her arms around him in a fervent embrace, her concern melting into a passionate relief that he is indeed safe and unharmed. Her hug, intense and full of emotion, bridges the gap between fear and love, as if trying to heal the night's trauma with the sheer force of her presence.

"Megumi," Ryan begins, his voice barely above a whisper as he pulls back from the embrace to meet her eyes. His gaze is fixed, carrying the weight of the night's grim revelations. "We need to talk." The seriousness in his tone cuts through the warm ambiance of the apartment. He watches as confusion flickers across Megumi's face, replaced swiftly by a shadow of concern. She nods, a silent acknowledgment, as she guides him to the sofa. "What happened, Ryan? Where were you?" Her voice, usually so composed, trembles with the urgency of her questions. Ryan takes a deep breath, knowing the words he's about to utter might very well change everything.

Now seated on the couch, Ryan looks deeply into Megumi's eyes, ".. and that's the plan." Megumi nods knowingly. "I was afraid this was coming."

Megumi reaches up and strokes Ryan's face as she looks deeply into his eyes, "We can leave. Let's just go to America and get married. We can build a new life there and you won't have to do this." Ryan's hand comes up to meet hers, "We can't run. I have to do this."

Megumi shakes her head, "No, no. You cannot do this. You are not like them." Ryan nods his head yes, "I have to. I gave Ishida my word." Megumi is dumbfounded, "Your word? What about the promises you made me? You will go to prison.. or worse? I can't let that happen." Ryan tries to calm her, "We have a plan. The plan will work. I have to do this."

Megumi shakes her head no, as tears well up in her eyes. "You can't. I don't care about any promises you may have made to Ishida. This is our life. I love you, and I cannot lose you. You understand that, right?" He nods yes as she continues, "Please promise me you won't do this." Ryan looks down as he silently nods.

He is nodding in agreement but in his heart he knows that he will do this. He has to. There is no other option.

Megumi reads the situation and takes a deep breath trying to regain her composure. She strokes his face and quietly says "I love you. I really do. I want us to have a long and happy life together. It's my past that got us into this."

She stands up and leaves the room without another word. Ryan sits on the couch in contemplation.

CHAPTER FIFTY-TWO
Thursday

To the outside observer, this was a Thursday like any other. The offices where Ryan and Megumi work are buzzing with activity, with the rank and file dutifully going about their days, giving their all to propel their company to new heights.

It's just after lunch time and Megumi is in her office, trying to concentrate on her work - which has amounted to an impossible task. Every thought is filled with Ishida and the dreadful action he is forcing Ryan to take.

Megumi resigns herself to an inability to concentrate and get anything done, she leans back in her chair and closes her eyes. There is a quick knock at the door and Ryan enters. Megumi is shocked at her sudden visitor and she tries to give Ryan a smile, but he sees right through it. Ryan looks happy, almost excited, "I've got it."

Megumi raises her eyebrows and Ryan continues, "I found somebody who can help. An outsider. They aren't known here. They are going to do it." Although Megumi is happy and relieved, she is also confused. "Who? How?" Ryan ignores her question, as he makes her way back behind her desk and kneels beside her and looks deeply into her eyes. "I see what this is doing to you. I don't want this to be a cloud over our special day. Just consider it handled." Megumi still presses for more information on this mystery savior. "Who did you find?" Ryan smiles, "I got in touch with an old friend from college. He knows a guy. It's all set up." Megumi continues to press, "Ishida is good with this?" Ryan nods, "All he said is that it can't be somebody known to the Yakuza or the Police. He will be good with it." Megumi sighs deeply and gives Ryan a smile that reflects a release of the dread and worry she has been carrying. Ryan gives her a warm smile, "I just saw what this was doing to you and there was no way I wanted that hanging over us on Saturday." She peers deeply into Ryan's eyes, "You have no idea how much better I feel. I love you so much."

Ryan takes her hands and looks deeply into Megumi's eyes, "I love you too. I need to get back to work. Lots to get done before Saturday." Megumi nods. Ryan gets up and leaves the office. Megumi takes a deep breath and looks up to the ceiling with a look of pure relief. After re-focusing, she leans back in to her computer and refocuses on her work with a renewed sense of purpose and clarity.

CHAPTER FIFTY-THREE

Friday Night

Under the soft glow of the restaurant's vintage chandeliers, Megumi and Ryan found themselves in an intimate booth, the world around them fading into the background. It was the evening before their wedding, a night suspended in the golden aura of anticipation. As they shared a quiet dinner, their conversation meandered through the landscapes of memories, laughter, and the occasional reflection.

Ryan reached for Megumi's hand across the table, his touch gentle and reassuring. "You know, tomorrow, when you walk down the aisle, it's going to be the start of our greatest adventure yet," he said with a tender smile.

Megumi's eyes shone with the same warmth as the candle on their table. "Our life together has already been an adventure, and I can't wait to see where it leads from here," she replied, her voice soft yet brimming with excitement.

The clinking of glasses and the distant hum of other patrons seemed to orchestrate a serenade to their prenuptial reverie. They savored their meals and each other's company, knowing that the next time they sat down to dinner, they would be doing so as a married couple.

Ryan and Megumi are sharing a chuckle as Kazu approaches the table. They greet him with a smile, which he returns to both his sister, and his very soon to be brother-in-law. He seems to be on edge and Megumi notices, "You okay?" Kazu nods, and turns his look to Ryan. "Do you have a minute to talk.. in private?" Ryan nods and excuses himself from the table. The two make their way down a nearby hallway and out of sight.

Standing in the hushed ambiance of the hallway, Kazu exuded a sense of formality and respectability that seemed to be worlds apart from the vibrant and audacious fabrics that once draped his frame during his Yakuza days. Gone were the ostentatious suits that commanded attention with their ornate patterns and glaring colors, replaced now by the understated elegance of dark tailored lines and the subtle sheen of a high-quality silk tie. His hair, once worn long and wild, was now meticulously styled in a conservative cut fitting for a boardroom. This transformation from flamboyant gangster to a polished businessman was marked not only in attire but in the calm, measured demeanor he presented—a mirror to the cultural expectations of Japan's corporate echelons. Just under the surface though, Kazu was still dangerous, as the steely glare in his eyes reflected as he glared at Ryan. "No outsiders. You understand?"

Ryan studies Kazu for a long moment before replying, "I understand." Kazu looks around the hallway to make sure nobody was listening in, "What's this I hear about an outsider doing the job tomorrow?" It's now Ryan's turn as he surveys the hallway with a look. "I'm doing it. Don't tell your sister." Kazu is processing this as Ryan glares back at him. Kazu takes a deep breath, "That isn't what I heard."

Ryan gathers his thoughts, "Look, your sister is the love of my life. I live for her, and I would gladly die for her. The one thing I cannot do is ruin her wedding day with this hanging over her. When we get up to say our vows, I don't want this hanging over her head. I want her to enjoy it.

You understand?"

Kazu nods, "So it was all bullshit? That you found somebody else?" Ryan nods, "Yes. I am meeting Ishida tomorrow just after the ceremony to get the instructions and I am taking care of it. Personally."

Kazu studies Ryan and takes a deep breath, "So you are lying to my sister?"

Ryan's look and posture turns deadly serious as he steps forward leaning into Kazu, "I am lying to your sister to not ruin her wedding. I am lying to your sister to deliver on a debt that Ishida is forcing me to pay back. I am lying to your sister because she is the only person I have ever loved, and I want to get her out of this bullshit nightmare world that you people operate in. I am doing this, and then I am done with it. Done with all of it. You tell her one fucking word and I will kill you first. You understand?"

Kazu nods begrudgingly, "I told Oyabun that I wanted to do it. That I owed you my life. He wouldn't let me." Ryan nods, "You are right. You do owe me. You owe us. The way you pay that back is by keeping your mouth shut. Understand?" Kazu nods. With his trademark sneer, he pats Ryan on the shoulder, "Good luck tomorrow."

Megumi is sitting at the table. She sees Ryan walking back to the table, and Kazu leaving without another look. Megumi asks Ryan, "Is everything okay?" Ryan takes a deep breath and sits down. He forces a smile, "Yeah, everything is fine."

Megumi studies Ryan's face and Ryan gives her a reassuring look, "It's fine." She believes him and she moves on, a genuinely happy smile on her face. "I can't wait for our honeymoon. Sitting on a beach, just us, just relaxing and enjoying life."

Her words trail off into the distance as Ryan thinks about the lie he is telling her. He hopes that everything goes smoothly - the wedding, the job he has to do, everything. Ryan wishes he could fast forward twenty-four hours from now and be in Hawaii - married, safe, and free from his obligation he has to fulfill tomorrow. The allure of the Yakuza he felt just a few nights prior has fully dissipated.

CHAPTER FIFTY-FOUR
Wedding Day

Megumi took her first step down the aisle, each movement an elegant testament to the journey that led here. Ryan, standing tall by the makeshift altar, felt a surge of emotion as he watched her approach. The sun, beginning its descent toward the horizon, cast a golden glow that seemed to favor them both, anointing this moment with a heavenly light. Around fifty guests, comprised of family and close friends, rose from their seats, their eyes fixed upon her silhouette.

The outdoor setting was a seamless blend of cultures—paper lanterns swayed alongside strings of white lights, and cherry blossoms met with delicate roses to form an arc of unity overhead. The sound of the ocean's waves, faithfully accompanying the special occasion, added a soothing rhythm to the soft music playing in the background.

As Megumi moved closer, every step she took was light, unfettered by the gravity of the world beyond the shores. Ryan, captured by the serenity of her smile, felt the weight of his resolve. For today, the past and future battles faded into the shimmering backdrop of the sea, affirming the present moment as something sacred and untouched.

As Megumi reached the final step, Ryan extended his hand, and she took it, completing the journey to his side with a grace that left the crowd in awe. The officiant's voice, warm and steady, began to guide them through the vows—a symbolic gateway to their shared future. Words were poised on Ryan's tongue, ready to pledge his love and life to Megumi, when his attention flickered. In the back row sat Ishida, his presence cutting through the serenity of the scene. Their eyes met. Ryan's pulse quickened, not with the anticipated nerves of a groom, but with the rush of understanding. Ishida, embodying the life Ryan was leaving behind, nodded once—a silent message understood only by those entangled in a world cloaked in shadows. As he stood and walked out of sight, Ryan felt a cold shiver of premonition amidst the warmth of the sun; a certainty that the past was never just a memory but a shadow always trailing just one step behind.

Ryan quickly refocused his gaze upon Megumi, her eyes glimmering with a constellation of promises and dreams. Drawing a deep breath, he let the waves' soft lull bring him back to the here and now. Their hands clasped together, he began to speak, his words flowing smoothly, laced with the heartfelt emotion of a love both deep and true. Megumi's voice then joined his, a harmonious echo, their vows painting a future of unwavering support and shared adventures. In that moment, the world beyond the venue ceased to exist; there was only Ryan and Megumi, the sea, the sky, and the unspoken oath to face whatever shadows may come, united and unbreakable.

As the final vows were tenderly exchanged, the officiant proclaimed them man and wife with a joyous authority that seemed to resonate with the very air around them. "You may now kiss the bride," he announced, to the elation of all gathered. Their kiss was a passionate crescendo, a fitting seal to the vows they had just pledged. Amidst the thunderous applause, they lingered in the kiss, an unspoken promise that every future triumph and trial would be shared from this day forward. As they slowly parted, locking themselves in a gaze that promised eternity, a gentle, yet insistent tug of urgency anchored Ryan back to the present. Somewhere beyond this moment of joy, Ishida's silent warning echoed in his mind. Now, more than ever, Ryan knew he needed to find him. But in the soft fold of Megumi's happiness, he masked his concern with a smile, determined not to cast a shadow on their day. He needed to find Ishida—and he would do so with care, ensuring Megumi remained unaware and undisturbed by the undercurrents of his past.

The reception buzzed with jubilant conversations and laughter as Ryan and Megumi navigated the maze of congratulatory hugs and handshakes. Their smiles never dulled as they gracefully accepted the well-wishes from family and friends. Yet, in the midst of this revelry, Ryan's mind was elsewhere; the need to find Ishida gnawed at him with increasing insistence. Seizing a moment when the music swelled and Megumi was swept away in celebratory conversations with her friends, Ryan excused himself to refresh their drinks. With a reassuring smile to Megumi, he edged through the crowd, his departure unnoticed by all but the keenest eyes. He slipped out of the main hall, the muffled sounds of celebration behind him quickly replaced by the silence of the corridor, where he hastened to uncover the whereabouts of Ishida.

Ryan briskly entered the lobby, his eyes swiftly scanning the room until they settled on the wedding planner, coordinating the evening's events with poised efficiency. As he approached, she looked up, her practiced smile briefly flitting to one of curiosity at the sight of the groom unaccompanied.

"Excuse me," Ryan interjected gently, careful to keep urgency from his voice, "have you seen Ishida-san around?"

Her expression shifted to one of recall, and after a brief moment, she nodded. "Yes, Ishida was here earlier. He seemed quite engaged in a discussion with Megumi-san's brother. Kazu-san I believe?"

With practiced subtlety, she continued, "They spoke for a while, and then I believe they both left together. They might be outside, or in the gardens, perhaps?"

A soft thank you was all Ryan offered before turning towards the entryway, the information provided both a lead and a new surge of worry. Why had Ishida left with Kazu? What were they discussing? The questions chased him as he stepped out, his resolve hardening with each stride. The search for Ishida had taken an unexpected turn, and Ryan intended to follow it to the end.

Ryan reached into his jacket, retrieving his cell phone with a swift motion, and dialed Kazu's number. The line rang, cutting through the hushed sounds of the night garden with its persistent tone. Once, twice, it rang—and then continued, unanswered, reverberating in the empty space around him. With each ring, Ryan felt the grip of tension tightening; no answer came. The call eventually surrendered to voicemail, leaving him with more questions than before. A frown creased his forehead as he pocketed the phone, his concern deepening under the weight of silence. He knew then that his next steps must be decided swiftly and with care.

Persisting, Ryan redialed Kazu's number, his fingers tapping a rapid, anxious rhythm against the side of his phone. Again, the trill of the ringtone cut through the stillness, a stark contrast to the whispering leaves in the night breeze. The sharp sense of panic that had been creeping into the edges of his thoughts was clawing its way forward, threatening to take hold. Just as the last vestiges of composure began to fray, a familiar figure emerged from the shadowed path — Ishida. With an appearance as sudden and silent as the night itself, Ishida's approach broke the cycle of unanswered calls and Ryan's mounting desperation.

"I am glad I found you. Do you have the instructions?" Ishida nods and hands Ryan a small envelope. With a steely nod, Ishida exclaims, "Congratulations to you and Megumi-san on your wedding. Please tell her I said congratulations?" Ryan nods, "Of course. Thank you for coming." With that, Ishida leaves and Ryan goes back out to see his guests momentarily before leaving on his murderous mission.

Ryan approached Megumi, her face illuminated by the soft glow of lanterns that adorned the periphery of the celebration. She was radiant, a picture of elegance and joy in her traditional wedding attire. But as she looked into Ryan's eyes, the ebullient sparkle in hers gave way to concern.

"Where's Kazu? I thought he'd be right behind you," Megumi asked, her voice tinged with expectation.

Ryan faltered for a moment, the absence of her brother casting a pall over his thoughts. "I... don't know," he admitted, feeling a mixture of concern and curiosity swirling within. He had expected Kazu to be part of their special day, and now his mysterious departure loomed ominously within Ryan's thoughts.

Ryan looks around. You are going to be good here for a few minutes? I need to pop back home and pick something up. Megumi's eyes narrow with the realization that Ryan's substitute for the Yakuza hit may have fallen through, "No, wait. Please don't go." Ryan kisses her on the cheek and starts to leave. Megumi stands frozen.

Ryan makes his way into the lobby when Megumi appears behind him, calling out, "Ryan?" Ryan stops and takes a look at his beautiful bride Megumi. He watches her intently as she approaches. In his mind, he is hoping that this isn't the last time he sees her. She approaches, a look of desperation on her beautiful face, "Please, don't go." Ryan takes a deep breath, "I have to. I'll be back as soon as I can. Spend time with your friends. Okay?" He turns to leave and she grabs his arm, "Please, don't go." Ryan pulls away and makes for the lobby door. He turns to see her one last time, "I love you. I'll be right back." With that, Ryan disappears from sight and out into the driveway area.

Megumi has a pit in her stomach that this may be the last time she sees her new husband.

CHAPTER FIFTY-FIVE
Hits and Misses

Ryan is riding in the back of a black taxi cab, feeling the hum of the city rhythm as it threads its way through Tokyo's ceaseless traffic. The world outside is a blur of neon kanji and corporate logos, all drowned in the cacophony of urban life. Clutched on his lap is a worn brown messenger bag, an inconspicuous companion holding a daunting secret. Inside, a .45 automatic pistol rests heavily against the worn fabric, its cold steel a stark contrast to the chaos outside. Ryan runs his fingers over the weapon, allowing the cool touch to calm his fraying nerves. Every vibration of the car seems to echo the tumult in his heart, each turn an unwelcome reminder that there is no turning back now.

The taxi driver casts a fleeting glance at Ryan via the rearview mirror, noting the beads of sweat furrowing down his passenger's forehead. Ryan has changed out of his tuxedo in favor of something more casual; the crisp lines of a tuxedo swapped for the nondescript simplicity of jeans paired with a hoodie. To any onlooker, Ryan could easily be mistaken for an American tourist caught in the rush of being late for a dinner appointment, an everyday occurrence in the bustling metropolis that scarcely warrants a second thought. Yet, underneath the facade, the gravity of Ryan's situation weighs upon him, invisible and heavy as the gun that lies dormant in his bag.

"How long until we get there?" Ryan asks, his voice barely concealing the tremor of nervousness. The taxi driver shakes his head, his eyes reflecting years of experience navigating this unpredictable concrete jungle. "Heavier traffic than usual," he mutters, the phrase hanging in the air like an unwelcome omen. Ryan feels a twinge in his gut, understanding that each second ticking by is a second less to act, to prepare. His gaze drifts back to the window, watching as life in Tokyo surges around him, oblivious to the turmoil that's unfolding in the back seat of this ordinary taxi cab.

The taxi abruptly rounds a corner and comes to an immediate stop; ahead, a chaotic scene unfolds as police barricades block the road, with officers flitting between vehicles, their faces stern and focused. Yellow tape flutters in the wind, marking the perimeter of a tragedy that has spilled onto the street. Ryan's heart stutters, the implications of such a blockade manifest clear as glass. Through the windshield, he sees a police officer approach, her hand resting on her holster in a gesture that speaks of routine caution and control.

The taxi driver, sensing a delay that can't be bypassed, rolls down his window with a resigned sigh. "What happened, officer?" he asks, attempting to mask his impatience with a veneer of concern. The officer, eyes scanning the interior of the cab, responds with practiced calm, "There's been an incident. Two yakuza groups decided to settle their scores. Ended in a shootout, and we've got multiple people dead." Her voice, although measured, carries the weight of the scene behind her. "It's going to be awhile before this clears up. You need to find an alternative route," she finishes, signaling the driver to turn around. Ryan knows what happened. Kazu stood in for him and the scene was an ugly one.

The driver, craning his neck to peer dubiously at the beleaguered street, then looks over his shoulder at Ryan, his brows furrowed with reluctance. "We're near your address; it's just one block up," he says, nodding toward the chaos, "You could walk it, if you're up to it. Not sure if the Police will let you through though." Ryan tries to swallow the knot of panic rising in his throat as he offers a tense nod of thanks to the driver. Agreeing to walk, he hastily pays his fare, fumbles with the door handle, and steps out from the stale warmth of the taxi into the brisk air, the echo of the melee at his back.

Ryan hoists the messenger bag, now heavy on his shoulder, a tangible weight of trepidation and urgency. As he distances himself from the taxicab, he casts a furtive glance towards the officers, praying silently that none challenge his passage. With each step, he tightens his grip on the strap of his bag, as if ensuring its contents remain a secret kept only by the leather and buckles. He hastens to the mouth of the block, the cacophony of sirens and orders fading with each hurried pace. Spotting a cab at the edge of the chaos, he waves it down with a brisk motion, sliding into the back seat as swiftly as he exited the first, giving the driver the address of the wedding venue. As the cab pulls away, the tinted windows obscure the scene, and in that fleeting moment of privacy, Ryan dares to hope that his cover remains intact.

Ryan's hand trembles slightly as he retrieves his cell phone from the inner pocket of his jacket. He stares at the screen for a tense second, Kazu's contact name glaring back at him. With a thumb hovering over the call button, a flurry of what-ifs race through his mind. He imagines Kazu's voice, the usual warm timbre now a dangerous liability. Pressing the screen to life, he's poised to dial, but with a last-minute surge of caution, he refrains. Any connection to Kazu's phone might be a thread for the police to unravel. With a sigh, Ryan locks the device and shoves it back into his jacket. The weight of unsent messages settles in the pit of his stomach as the cityscape blurs by.

Ryan slips into the lavishly decorated wedding venue, his tuxedo clinging to his skin and speckled with signs of his ordeal. Despite an attempt to pat down his unruly hair, it rebels at the temples, announcing his recent haste. Across the room, Megumi expertly navigates social niceties with their guests, her laughter a little too high-pitched, her glances towards the entrance a little too frequent. As his presence registers, her eyes lock onto his with a surge of relief that melts into her smile. She excuses herself with grace and crosses to Ryan. The couple's embrace is a silent exchange of worries and reassurances; her fingers threading through his hair, pressing the past hour into the folds of forgotten memories. Megumi peers into Ryan's eyes, "Are you okay?" Ryan nods, trying to be nonchalant in front of the guests who have barely noticed his re-appearance. "I'm good, but we need to take off." Megumi nods. She was expecting this. She takes his hand, "Come with me." She leads him up to the podium. She takes the microphone with the grace and poise of a true professional. She speaks into the microphone, "Everyone, thank you so much for coming today. As my husband has reminded me, we need to get to the airport so we don't miss our flight." She gives a practiced smile. Multiple guests raise their glasses in approval.

They quickly leave, making their way through the crowd of well wishers.

Inside Megumi's dressing room, the air bristles with the haste of departure. She swiftly exchanges her bridal gown for street attire—a pair of yoga pants, simple tennis shoes, and a snug hoodie. This ensemble, reminiscent of their early days, once captured Ryan's attention with its understated charm. Despite the present urgency, Ryan finds himself captivated by her beauty anew, an admiration that lingers in his gaze. She's a whirlwind of motion, barely registering his stare as she snatches up the last of her belongings. "Let's go," she urges, her voice a decisive cut through the bittersweet tension, signaling the end of ceremony and the start of something anew. Together, they slip out, leaving behind a trail of whispered goodbyes and unspent celebration.

CHAPTER FIFTY-SIX
Departures

Megumi and Ryan's taxi glides to a halt at Tokyo's Haneda Airport, disgorging the two into the bustling terminal with its steady hum of departure announcements and rolling suitcases. They navigate through the crowd, a silent agreement etched in their swift movements towards the ticketing window. The attendant hands them their boarding passes and the bittersweet flutter of their departure settles within as they make their way to security.

Passing through the scanners is a practiced dance of unloading pockets and removing shoes. Despite the routine, their senses are heightened, eyes scanning discreetly over the uniformed figures of police and airport security. They seek the slightest hint of unwanted attention, but find none. It's a strange solace, being invisible in plain sight, among travelers oblivious to their rush of emotions. With no barriers left, they step into the travelers' stream, moving toward their gate – and with each step, further from yesterday's whispered goodbyes.

As the Airbus lifts effortlessly into the Tokyo skyline, Megumi turns her attention to Ryan. He is a silhouette against the panoramic window, the city's lights casting a mosaic of shadows across his features. He seems entranced by the receding tapestry of Tokyo's gleaming streets and the muffled roar of the engines fills the space with an ambient hum. She leans closer and asks him if he's all right, searching for comfort in his presence. Ryan only nods, his eyes still locked on the diminishing world outside, harboring a storm of thoughts and feelings too tumultuous for words. His silent profile is a stark reminder of the weight they carry with them, soaring into the night sky and away from a life once known.

Megumi continues to study his face, "Did you.. do it?" Ryan looks to Megumi and gently shakes his head, "I didn't get a chance to." Megumi searches for understanding as he just looks at her, "I think that.. I think that. someone else did.. but I am not sure." The two share a look, not sure what this means. It's one thing to know,, and a completely other to not know the outcome. Given the situation, there is no way that Ryan can contact Ishida to find out."

Ryan and Megumi are seated side by side in their plush first class seats, separated by only a foot or so, but in their minds, they are worlds apart. Megumi's mind races through the consequences of Ryan not delivering on his mission while Ryan runs through imaginary scripts on how he will break the news to Megumi that her brother stepped in and took his place, and is almost surely dead.

Chapter Fifty-Seven

Hawaii

The Grand Hyatt on the island of Kauai looms impressively as Ryan and Megumi approach its welcoming embrace. The tropical air, scented with plumeria and the salty tang of the ocean, greets them as they step through the expansive lobby. At the check-in desk, an attendant offers warm Aloha smiles, efficiently handing them key cards encased in a decorative sleeve. They navigate through the elegantly adorned lobby, eyes tracing the intricate patterns of native artwork that line the walls.

The moment they open the door to their honeymoon suite, the breathtaking vista captivates them. The room is bathed in the soft golden hue of the late afternoon sun, and a gentle breeze whispers through the open lanai doors. The vast ocean stretches to the horizon, its waters shimmering under the waning sun. The suite is more than they had imagined—spacious, with a kind of understated luxury that speaks of serenity and privacy, the perfect refuge from their tumultuous past days. With a shared, silent understanding, they step onto the balcony, allowing the beauty of Kauai to envelop them, offering a temporary respite from the storms that lie within.

As they stand taking in the view, Ryan turns to Megumi, "I love you, and I hope you can forgive me for lying to you." Megumi looks down at her feet and back to Ryan, love filling her eyes, "It's me that should apologize. I brought you into this whole situation. I should have been more honest with you." Relief washes over Ryan as he smiles, "I love you. We are married. I wouldn't change one thing about you." Megumi continues, "You did what you did, or what you tried to do.. you did for us. I understand that." Ryan takes a deep breath, "I need to tell you something." Megumi stares at him intently. She reads the seriousness in his tone. Just as he is about to speak, there is a knock at the door. Ryan looks over to the door, but before he can move, Megumi makes her way over and opens it. A Hotel employee greets her with a smile, "Megumi McFarlane?" She nods, and the employee hands her an envelope, "This just arrived for you." She accepts it with a smile and the employee disappears down the hallway. She looks at Ryan with a smile, "Megumi McFarlane, I like the way that sounds." She opens the envelope as she walks back over to Ryan, who stands searching for the words to let her know that her brother stepped in for him and is now, almost surely, dead.

As Megumi walks, her delicate smile fades into a look of disbelief. As she continues to read, her eyes narrow. Ryan instinctively steps in. He touches her shoulder and she pulls away, her eyes stay riveted on the letter. Her eyes lock with Ryan's and she hands him the letter. As Ryan begins to read, she walks away, making her way to the other side of the suite, sliding the door open and stepping out on to the balcony.

Ryan reads the letter. After a long moment of contemplation, he sets the letter on the table and makes his way across the suite and out on to the balcony.

Ryan and Megumi are standing on the balcony. The scenic beauty of the moment is overshadowed by the feelings of loss and regret. Ryan reaches over and puts his hand on the small of her back. She continues to face forward, looking out at the ocean. "This is why we were never close. I knew this day would come." Ryan just nods. Megumi continues,

"I just can't believe he is gone." Ryan nods, he has no idea what to say. "Kazu was a very brave man. He did this for us." Ryan says as he tries to comfort her. Tears start to well up in her eyes, "Let's take a walk?" She asks. Ryan nods yes.

The sun is fading off in the horizon, and the sky is a beautiful mix of purples and pinks, highlighted by a few scattered clouds in the distance. Ryan and Megumi are walking barefoot on the beautiful sands, oblivious to a few kids still playing in the waves as their parents sit blissfully on the beach. This amazing scene is totally lost on Ryan and Megumi as they are deep in conversation.

Ryan stops walking and looks at Megumi. His eyes are filled with pain and regret, "I was going to be the one to do it, I promise you that." After taking a moment to steady herself, Megumi looks deeply into Ryan's eyes, her pain is hidden behind a wall of stoicism. "I know, but this was his destiny. He lived an honorable life. Or as honorable as any Yakuza could. For what it's worth he wanted to be a Samurai, and this was a very honorable end. This is how he would have wanted it." Ryan just nods.

Ryan's cell phone buzzes. He holds up the phone, "It's the hotel. My parents are here." Ryan answers it, "Yeah. Yeah, you can give them a key. Thank you." Ryan looks to Megumi, "I guess we should head back. Feel free to just go in and get a nap. I know this is a lot. I can hang out with them and get them settled in." She forces a smile. "I'll be okay. It will be great to see them."

Before they start to walk away, Megumi takes Ryan's hand, "Wait, let's just soak this in. Just for a moment." They turn to admire the sunset and they soak it in. Megumi puts her hands together and dips her head for a moment, "He is with us. He loves you and he did what he did for us, to protect us." Ryan fights back tears as he thinks back to Kazu and the wild ups and downs of their relationship. He nods and puts his hands together with a silent bow. "Thank you Kazu." Ryan adds.

The feeling of despair and loss hangs heavy in the otherwise beautiful hallway of the luxury hotel. Ryan and Megumi make their way up the hall toward their room. Ryan pulls out his keycard and looks to Megumi, "You good?" She nods stoically. He opens the door and the two enter the room, ready to greet Ryan's parents.

As they enter, their eyes widen and their jaws drop. Kazu is sitting on the couch. Megumi's expression turns to unbridled joy as she runs over to him. He stands from the couch and they lock in an enthusiastic hug. After a long moment, Megumi pulls back and looks at Kazu, her eyes still filled with disbelief and joy. "I thought you were dead!" He grins, "I should be." Ryan comes over and gives him a hug. Megumi continues, "The note? What was that about?"

Megumi steps back. Ryan and Megumi look at Kazu with disbelief. "I was on my way to do it. Yeah, I wasn't going to let you take the fall. Some of the guys heard about the plan and they wanted to keep it in the family. You're not a true Yakuza, Ryan." Ryan grins, "I was on my way and the roads were closed. Then we got your letter.."

Kazu nods, "The letter. Yeah. I guess things didn't go as planned."

Ryan is dumbfounded. "So... who did it?"

Kazu just nods. "Don't ask questions. All you need to know is that Oyabun knows you intended to do your duty. Your deal with him still stands. You... and your family will always be under our protection."

Megumi interjects, "Our protection? I thought you were done." Kazu nods, "It's the life I chose. Things are changing. Things are changing for the better and I got a promotion."

Ryan nods, "And your job with us?"

Ryan and Megumi study Kazu's reaction. Kazu looks down at the ground, "I appreciate all you have both done for me, but yes, please accept my resignation."

Megumi takes a deep breath, "I am just happy you are alive. I still have my little brother." Kazu grins. Ryan smiles and nods, "Me too. I am very happy to see you. And I am grateful you stepped in to pay my debt."

They all share a heartfelt and happy moment. The pain and chaos of the past two days have passed. Life is good.

There is a knock at the door. Ryan takes a deep breath and looks to Kazu and Megumi. He makes his way over to the door and opens it. Ryan's parents are standing there, all smiles. For the first time in what feels like an eternity, Ryan returns their smile with an authentic one of his own.

THE END

UPDATE

Shortly after dinner, later that night, Kazu boarded a flight back to Tokyo to resume his career with the Yakuza. He is now Ishida's second in command and doing very well. Profits are up and the turf wars have ended, bringing calm and order to the Tokyo underworld.

After enjoying a blissful honeymoon, Megumi and Ryan returned to Tokyo. Their company is thriving and all is well. They are expecting their first child in the Fall. With some help from Kazu and Ryan, Megumi has even mended the relationship with her father. Ryan, against all odds, has even been welcomed into her family. Her dad even thinks of Ryan as a son.

Despite the ups and downs, their love prevailed over all.

March 10th 2024